KICKLIY

THE MOUSE OF MONET

BOOKS

PEFC Certified

This product is from
sustainably managed
forests and
controlled sources.

PEFC
10-31-1800   pefc-france.org

ISBN 978-1-941250-09-9
First Edition, June 2016
Printed in France.

DISTRIBUTED TO THE TRADE BY
Consortium Book Sales & Distribution
LLC. 34 Thirteenth Avenue NE
Suite 101, Minneapolis, MN 55413-1007.
cbsd.com, Orders: (800) 283-3572

ododbooks.com

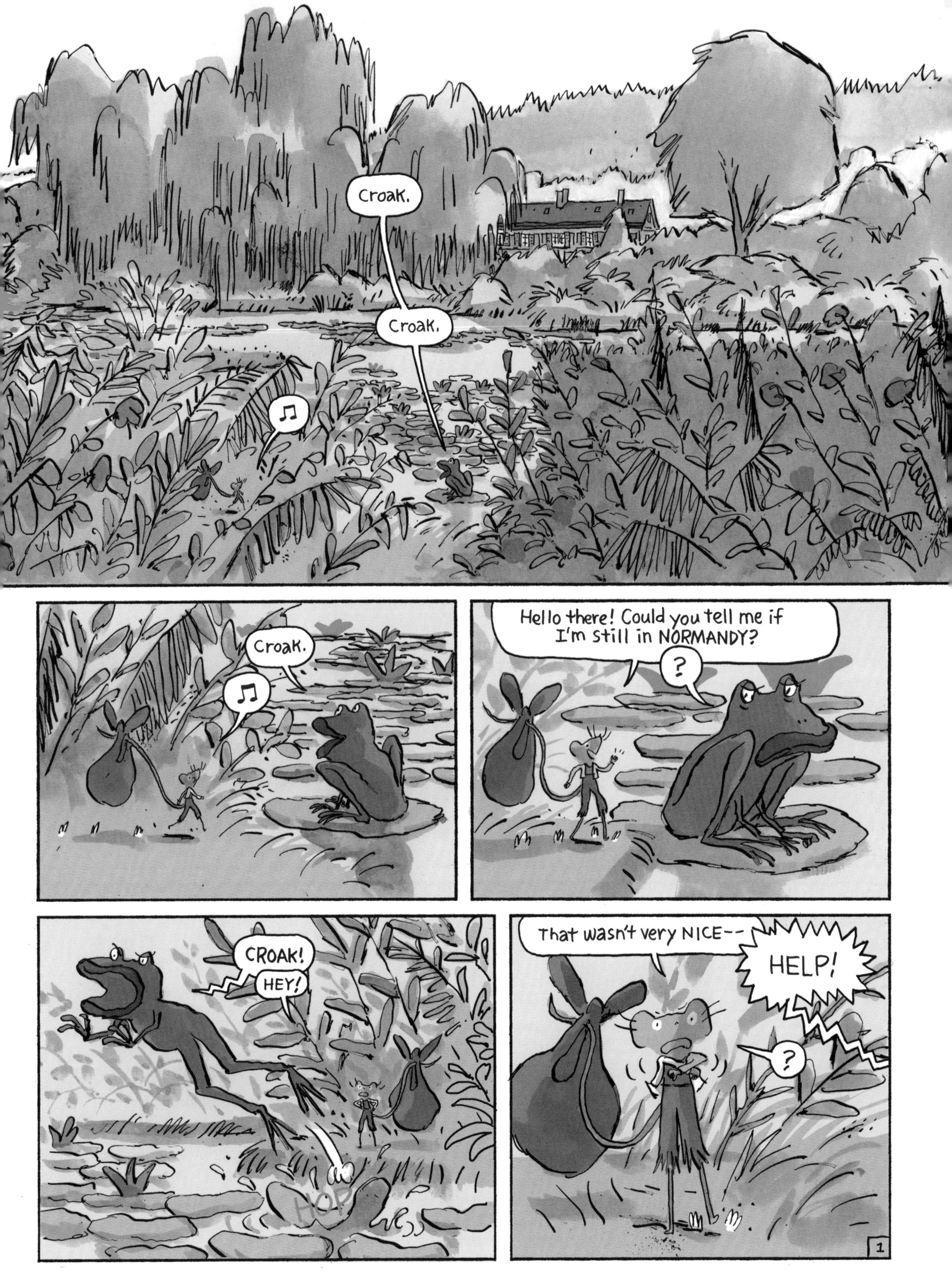
Croak.
Croak.
♫
Croak.
♫
Hello there! Could you tell me if I'm still in NORMANDY?
?
CROAK!
HEY!
HOP
That wasn't very NICE--
HELP!
?
1

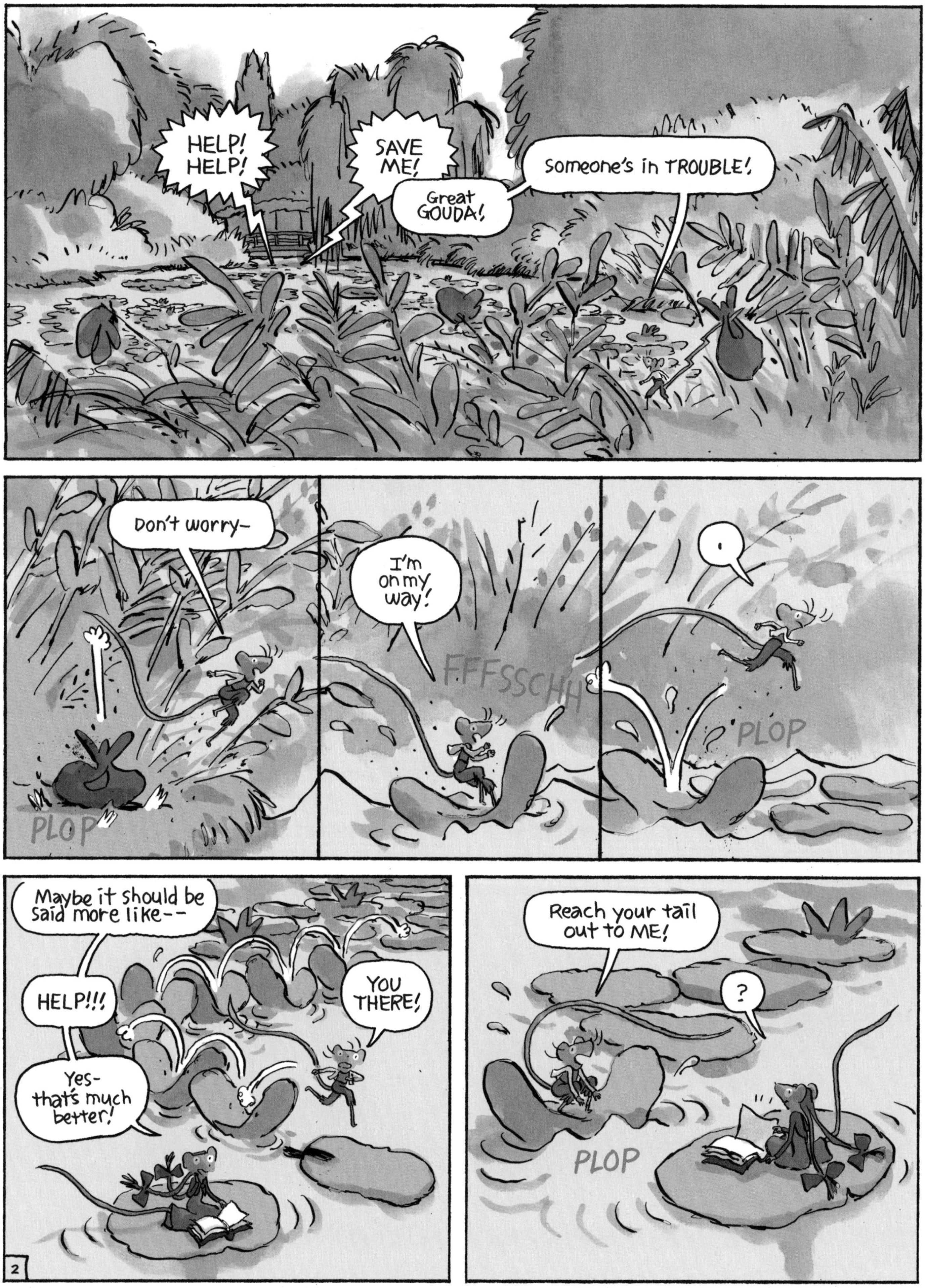
HELP! HELP!
SAVE ME!
Great GOUDA!
Someone's in TROUBLE!
Don't worry-
I'm on my way!
FFFSSCHH
PLOP
PLOP
Maybe it should be said more like--
HELP!!!
Yes- that's much better!
YOU THERE!
Reach your tail out to ME!
?
PLOP
2

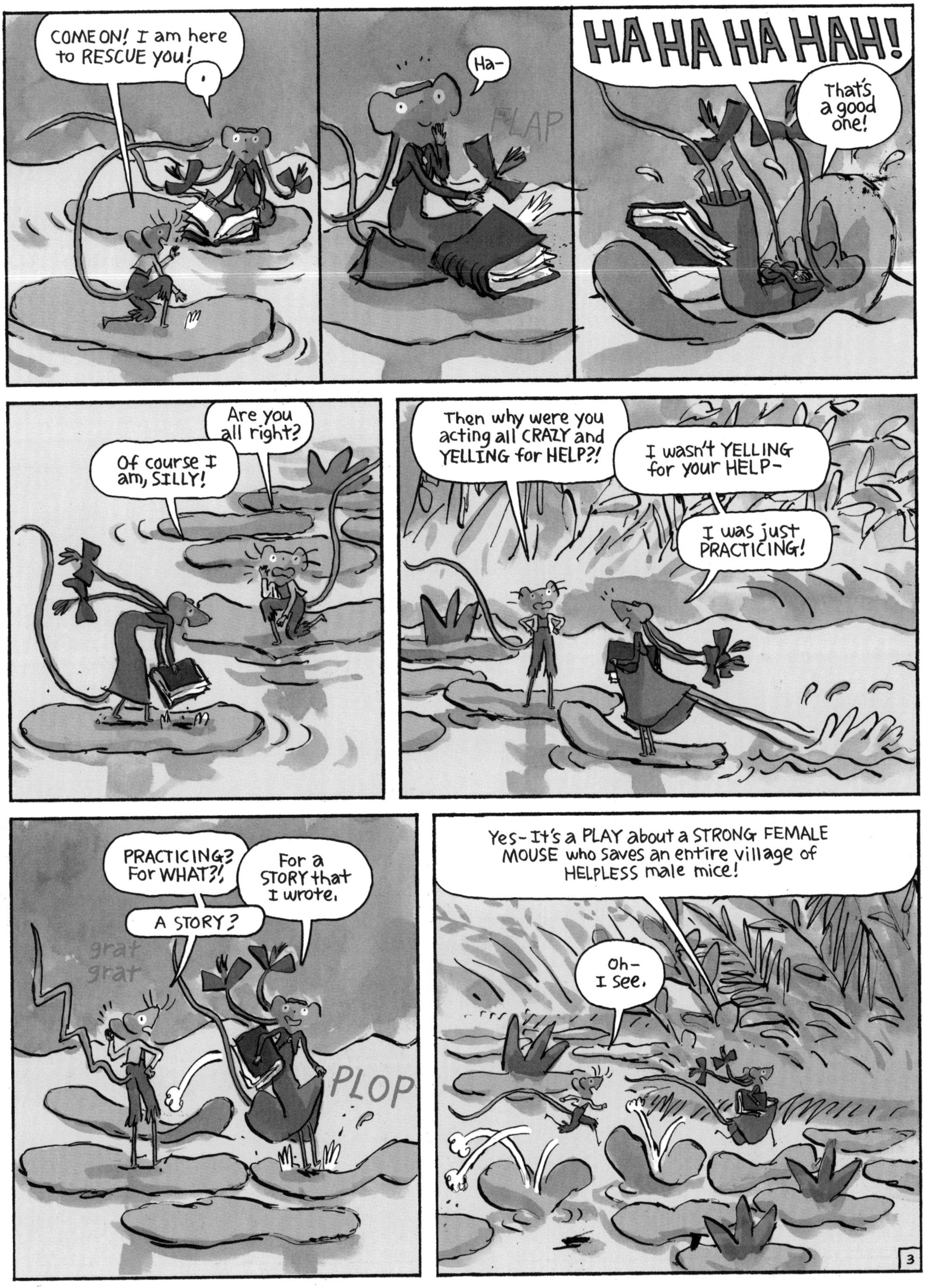
COME ON! I am here to RESCUE you!
Ha-
FLAP
HA HA HA HAH!
That's a good one!
Are you all right?
Of course I am, SILLY!
Then why were you acting all CRAZY and YELLING for HELP?!
I wasn't YELLING for your HELP-
I was just PRACTICING!
PRACTICING? For WHAT?!
For a STORY that I wrote.
A STORY?
grat grat
PLOP
Yes- It's a PLAY about a STRONG FEMALE MOUSE who saves an entire village of HELPLESS male mice!
Oh- I see.
3

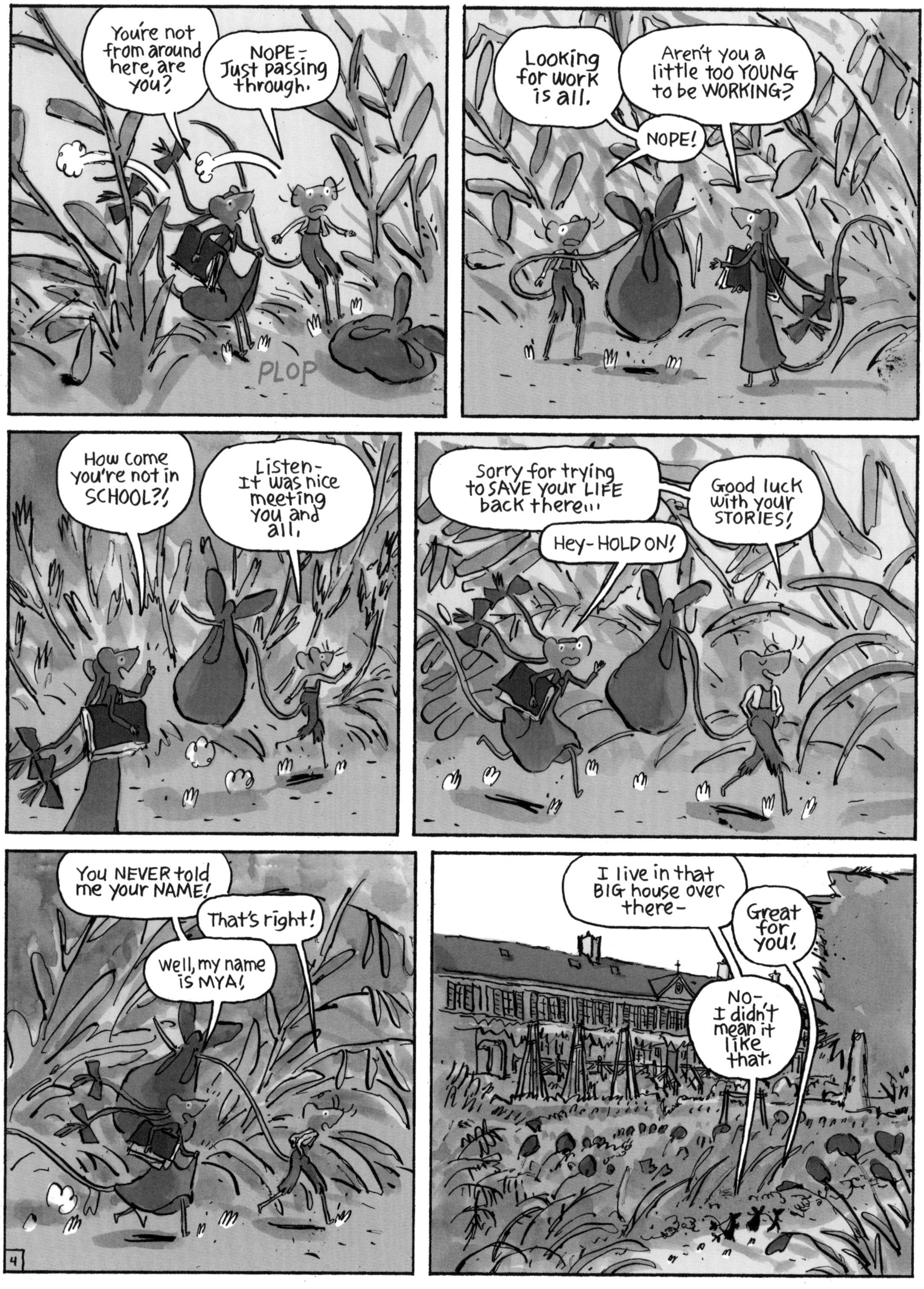
You're not from around here, are you?
NOPE- Just passing through.
PLOP
Looking for work is all.
Aren't you a little too YOUNG to be WORKING?
NOPE!
How come you're not in SCHOOL?!
Listen- It was nice meeting you and all.
Sorry for trying to SAVE your LIFE back there...
Good luck with your STORIES!
Hey- HOLD ON!
You NEVER told me your NAME!
That's right!
Well, my name is MYA!
I live in that BIG house over there-
Great for you!
No- I didn't mean it like that.

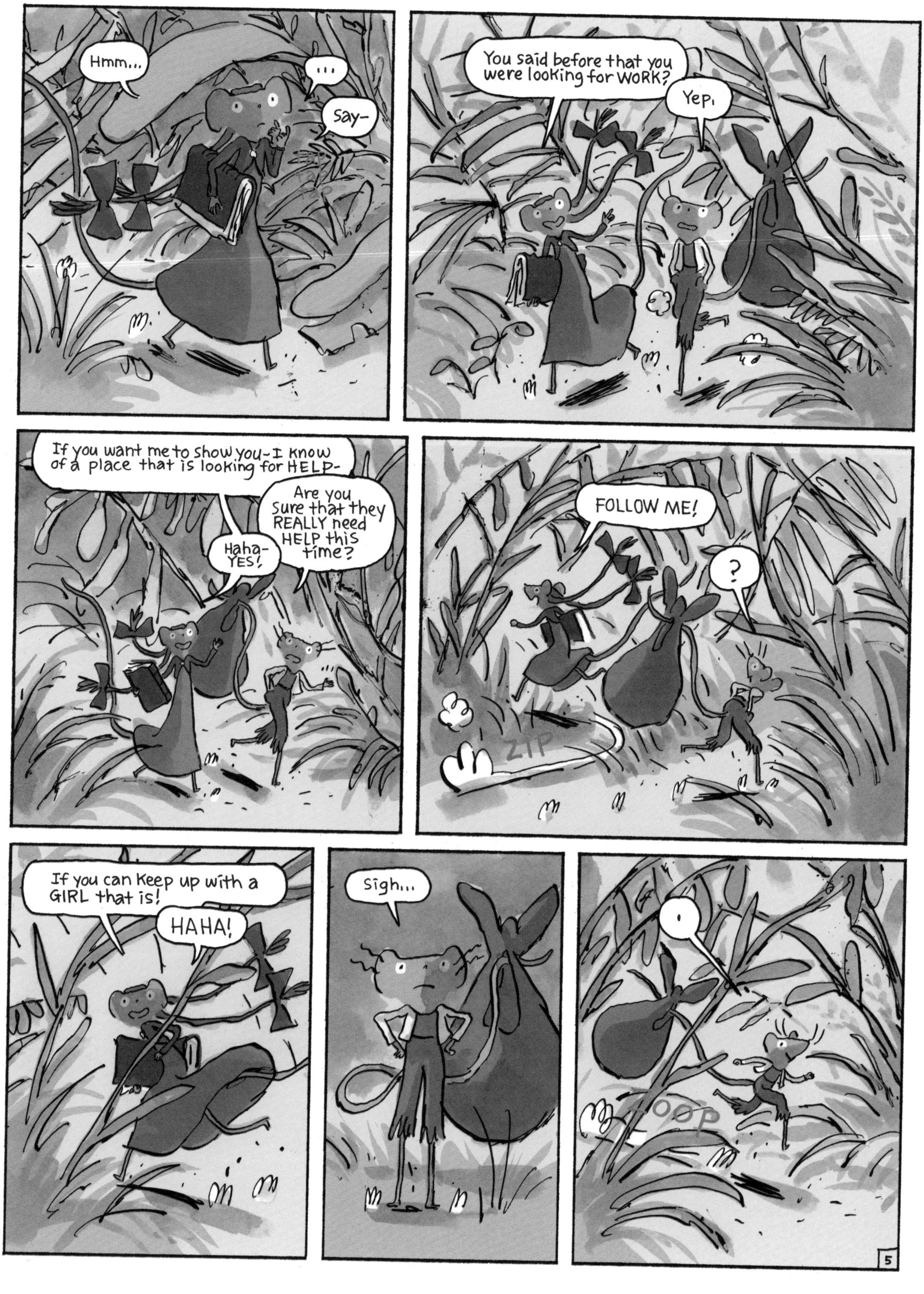
Hmm...
...
Say-
You said before that you were looking for WORK?
Yep.
If you want me to show you- I know of a place that is looking for HELP-
Haha- YES!
Are you sure that they REALLY need HELP this time?
FOLLOW ME!
?
ZIP
If you can keep up with a GIRL that is!
HAHA!
Sigh...
5

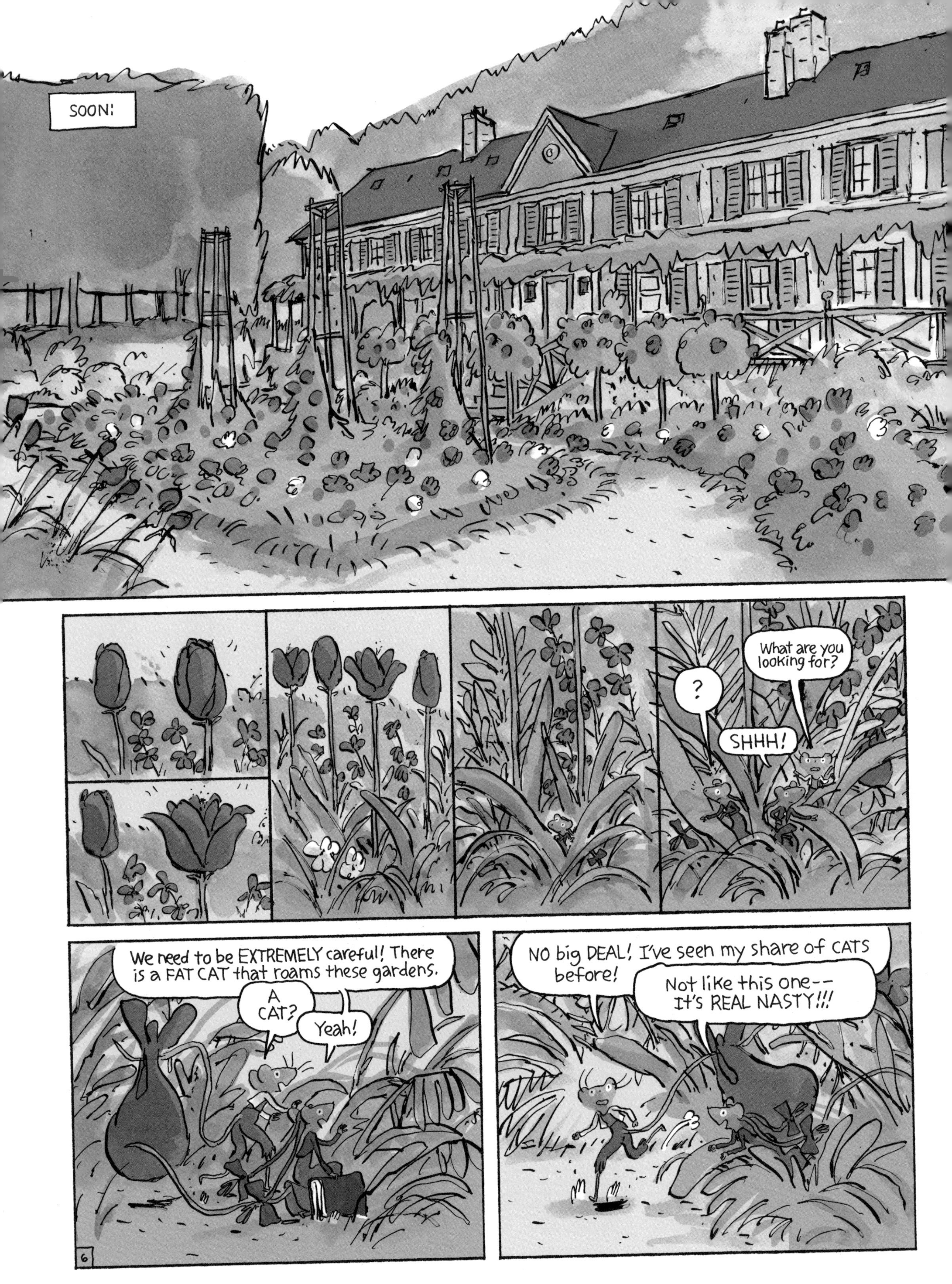

SOON:
What are you looking for?
?
SHHH!
We need to be EXTREMELY careful! There is a FAT CAT that roams these gardens.
A CAT?
Yeah!
NO big DEAL! I've seen my share of CATS before!
Not like this one-- It's REAL NASTY!!!
6

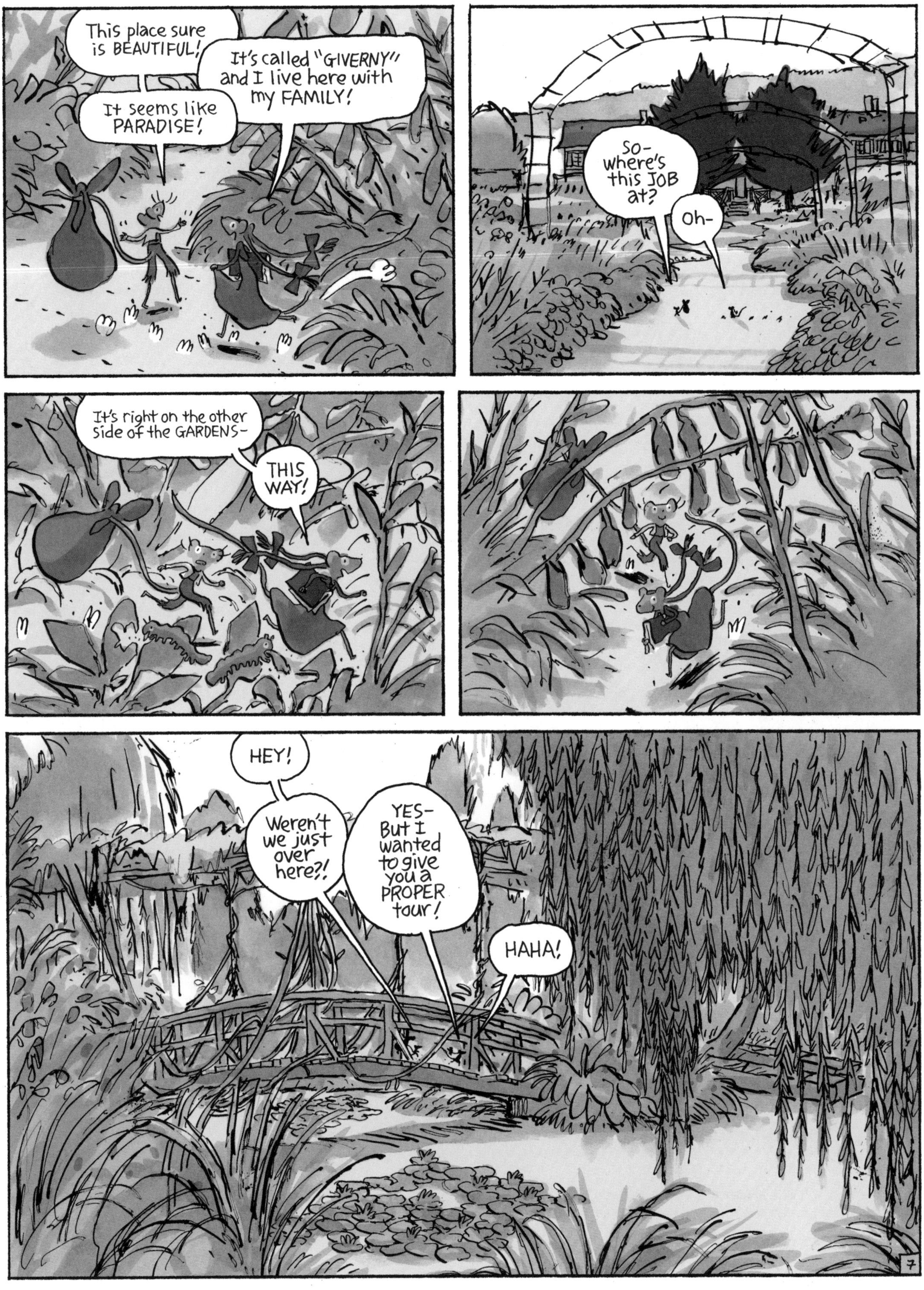
This place sure is BEAUTIFUL!
It seems like PARADISE!
It's called "GIVERNY" and I live here with my FAMILY!
So- where's this JOB at?
Oh-
It's right on the other side of the GARDENS-
THIS WAY!
HEY!
Weren't we just over here?!
YES- But I wanted to give you a PROPER tour!
HAHA!
7

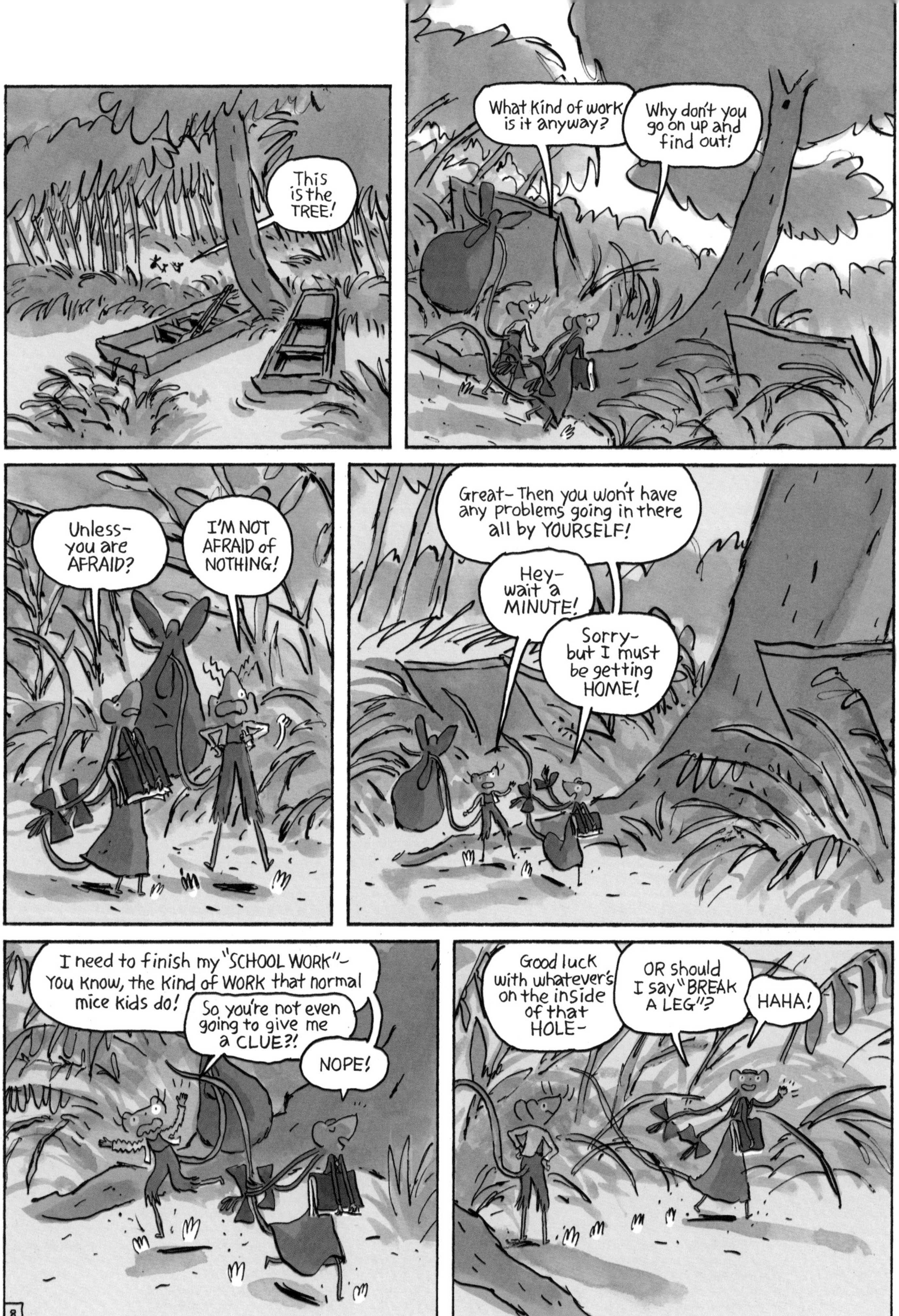
This is the TREE!
What kind of work is it anyway?
Why don't you go on up and find out!
Unless- you are AFRAID?
I'M NOT AFRAID of NOTHING!
Great- Then you won't have any problems going in there all by YOURSELF!
Hey- wait a MINUTE!
Sorry- but I must be getting HOME!
I need to finish my "SCHOOL WORK"- You know, the kind of WORK that normal mice kids do!
So you're not even going to give me a CLUE?!
NOPE!
Good luck with whatever's on the inside of that HOLE-
OR should I say "BREAK A LEG"?
HAHA!
8

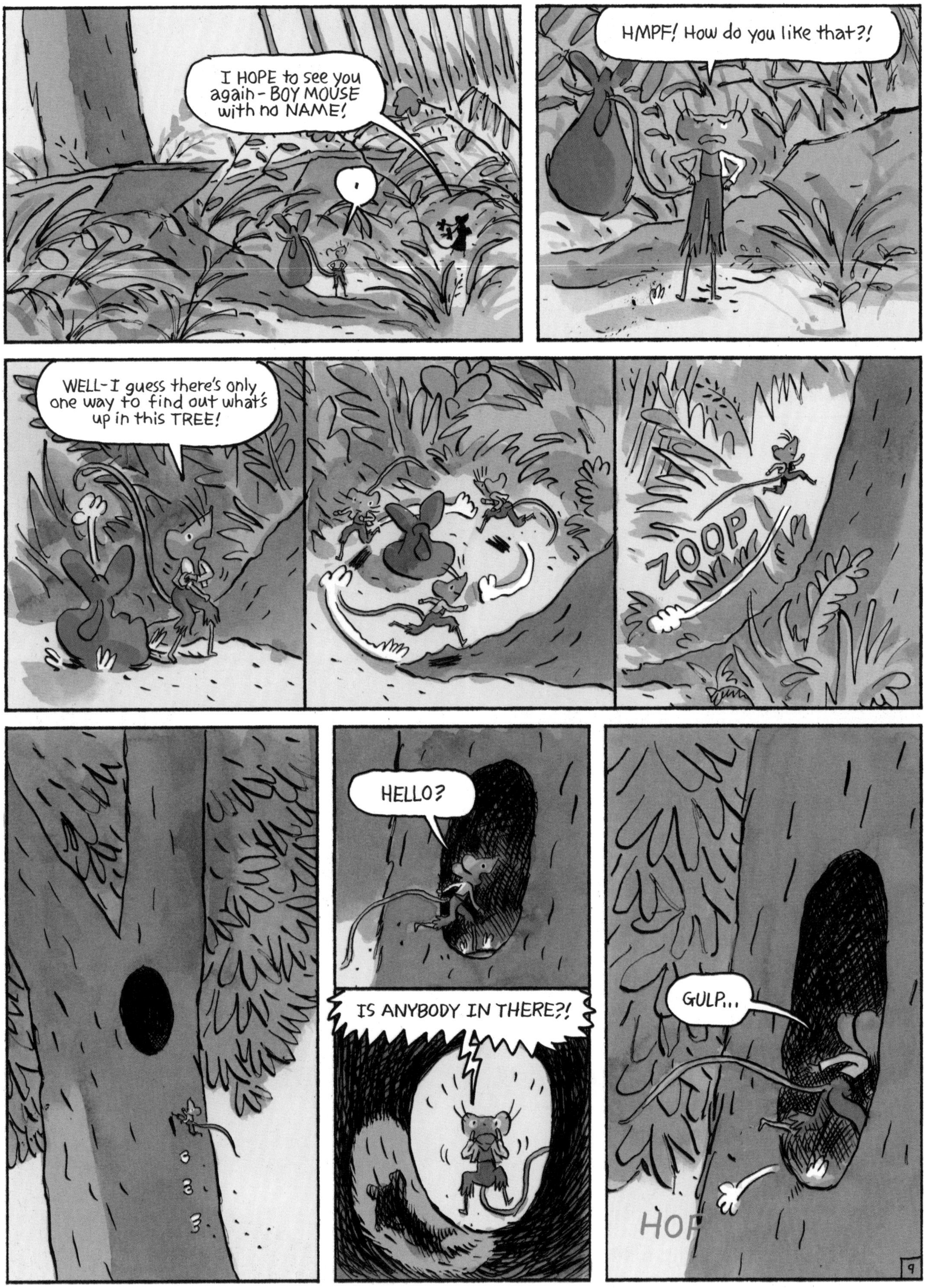
I HOPE to see you again - BOY MOUSE with no NAME!
!
HMPF! How do you like that?!
WELL- I guess there's only one way to find out what's up in this TREE!
ZOOP
HELLO?
IS ANYBODY IN THERE?!
GULP...
HOP
9

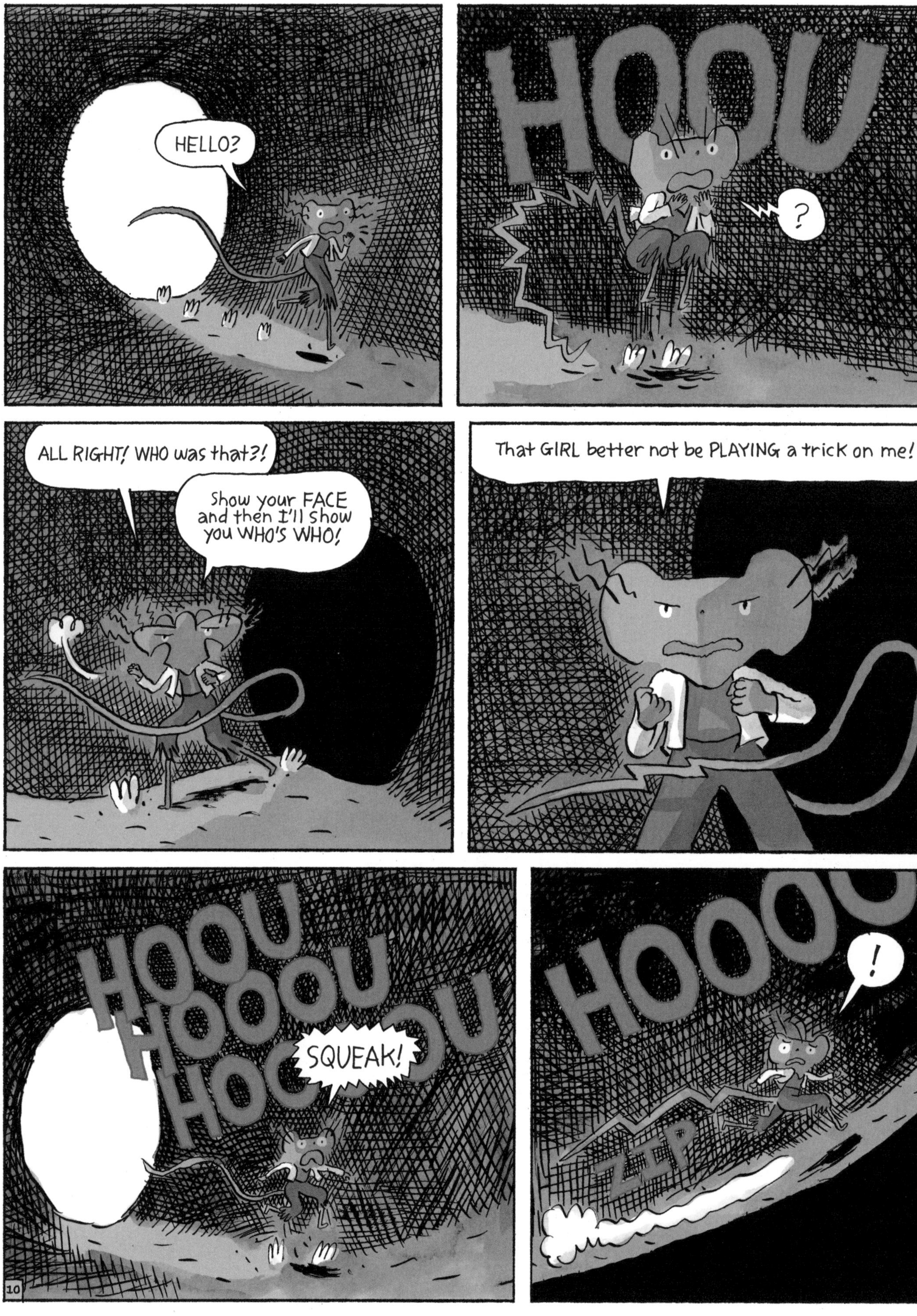
HELLO?
HOOU
?
ALL RIGHT! WHO was that?!
Show your FACE and then I'll show you WHO'S WHO!
That GIRL better not be PLAYING a trick on me!
HOOU
HOOOU
HOOOOU
SQUEAK!
10
HOOOO
!
ZIP

OOOU
?
CRASH
Oof!
What are you doing PESTERING me in my STUDIO?!
11

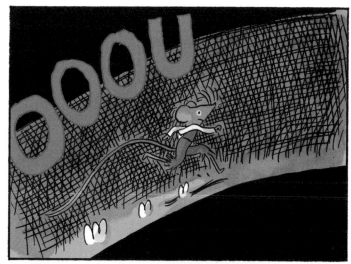

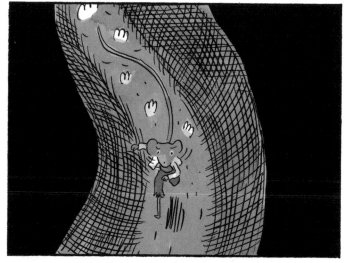

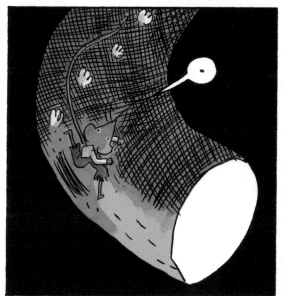

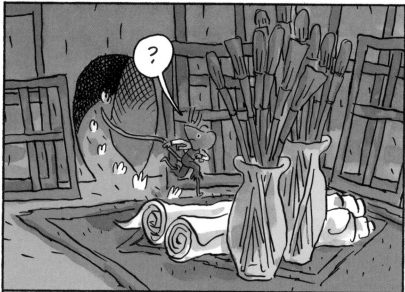

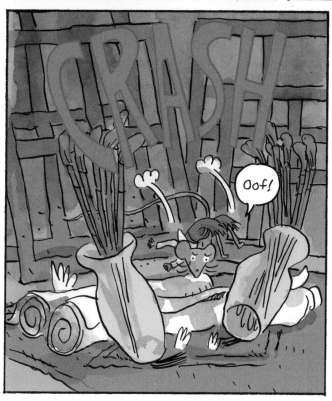

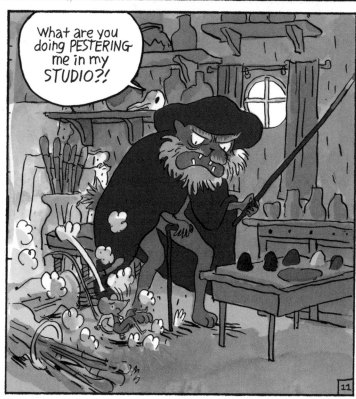

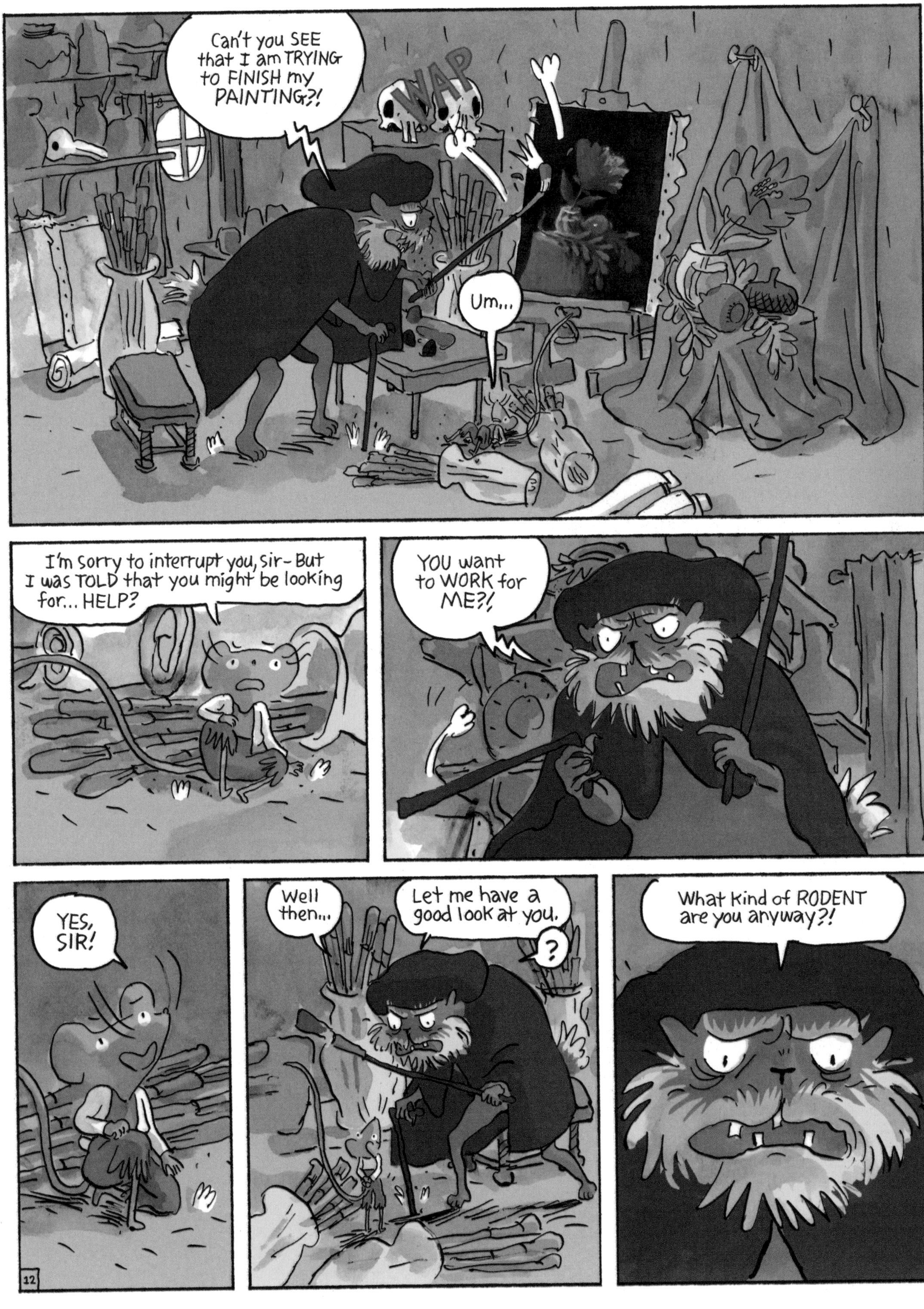
Can't you SEE that I am TRYING to FINISH my PAINTING?!
WAP
Um...
I'm sorry to interrupt you, sir- But I was TOLD that you might be looking for... HELP?
YOU want to WORK for ME?!
YES, SIR!
Well then...
Let me have a good look at you.
?
What kind of RODENT are you anyway?!
12

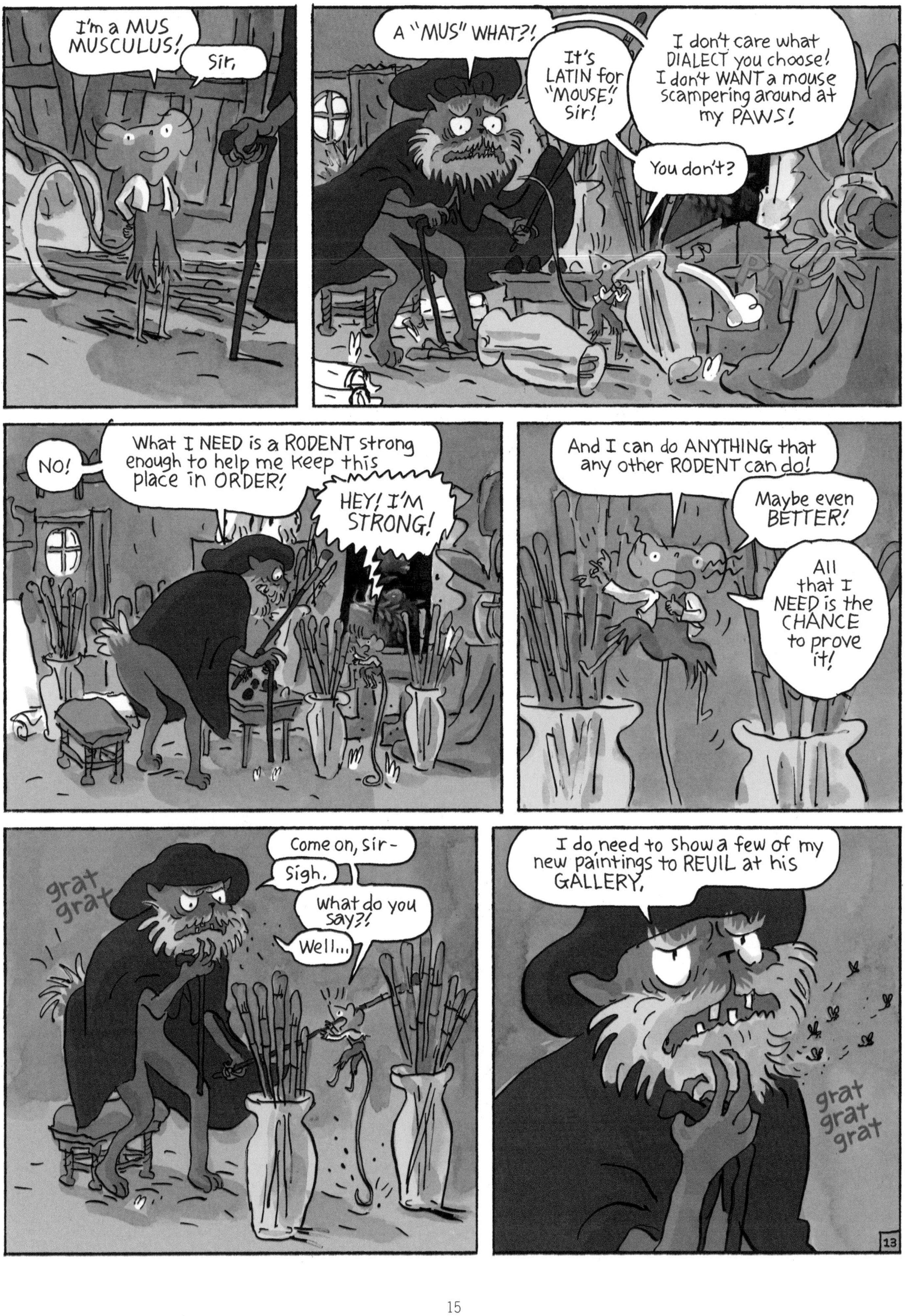
I'm a MUS MUSCULUS!
Sir,
A "MUS" WHAT?!
It's LATIN for "MOUSE," Sir!
I don't care what DIALECT you choose! I don't WANT a mouse scampering around at my PAWS!
You don't?
RIP
NO!
What I NEED is a RODENT strong enough to help me keep this place in ORDER!
HEY! I'M STRONG!
And I can do ANYTHING that any other RODENT can do!
Maybe even BETTER!
All that I NEED is the CHANCE to prove it!
grat grat
Come on, sir-
Sigh.
What do you say?!
Well...
I do need to show a few of my new paintings to REUIL at his GALLERY,
grat grat grat
13

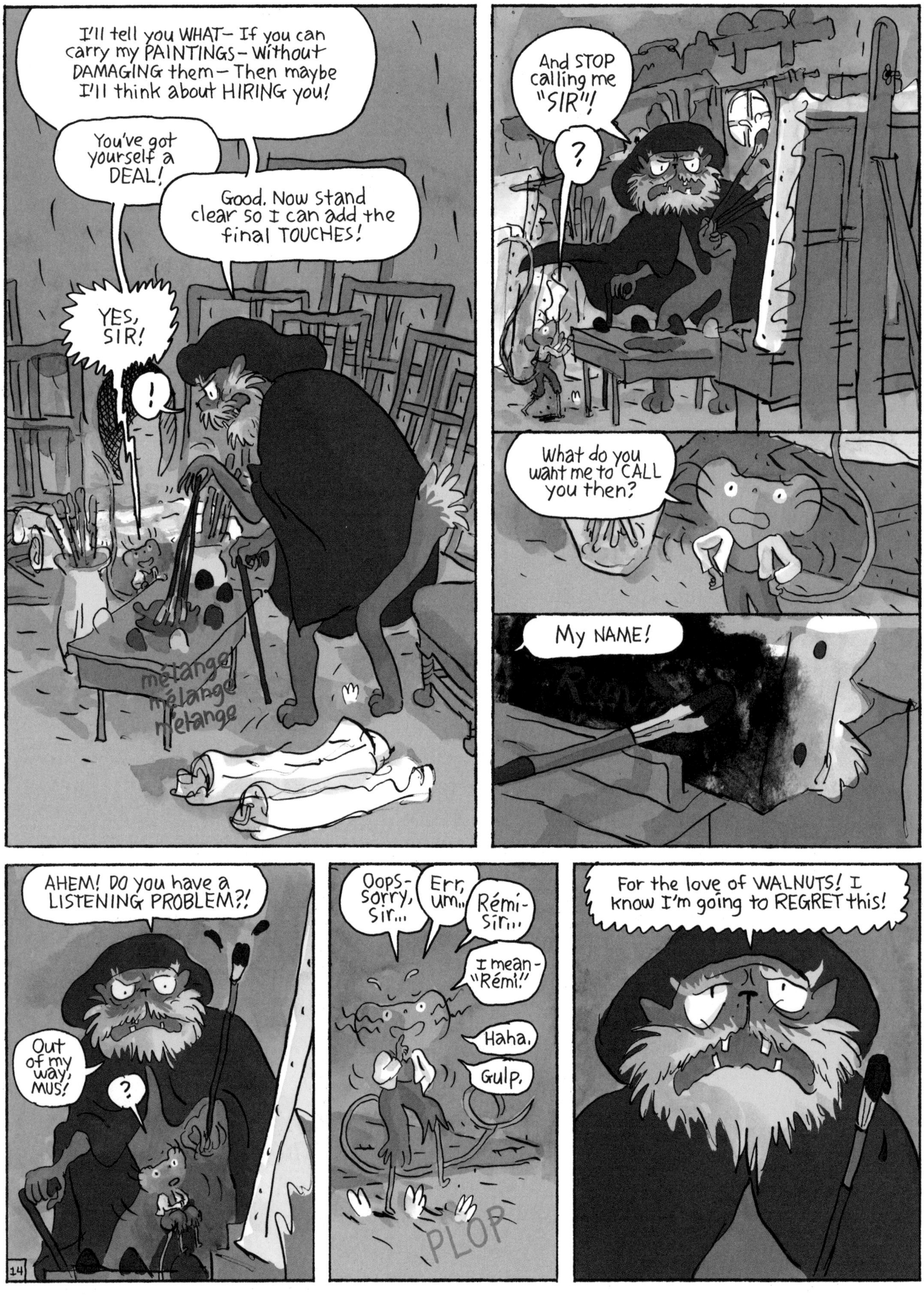
I'll tell you WHAT– If you can carry my PAINTINGS– Without DAMAGING them– Then maybe I'll think about HIRING you!
You've got yourself a DEAL!
Good. Now stand clear so I can add the final TOUCHES!
YES, SIR!
!
mélange mélange mélange
And STOP calling me "SIR"!
?
What do you want me to CALL you then?
My NAME!
AHEM! DO you have a LISTENING PROBLEM?!
Out of my way, MUS!
?
14
Oops-sorry, sir...
Err, um...
Rémi-sir...
I mean- "Rémi!"
Haha.
Gulp.
PLOP
For the love of WALNUTS! I know I'm going to REGRET this!

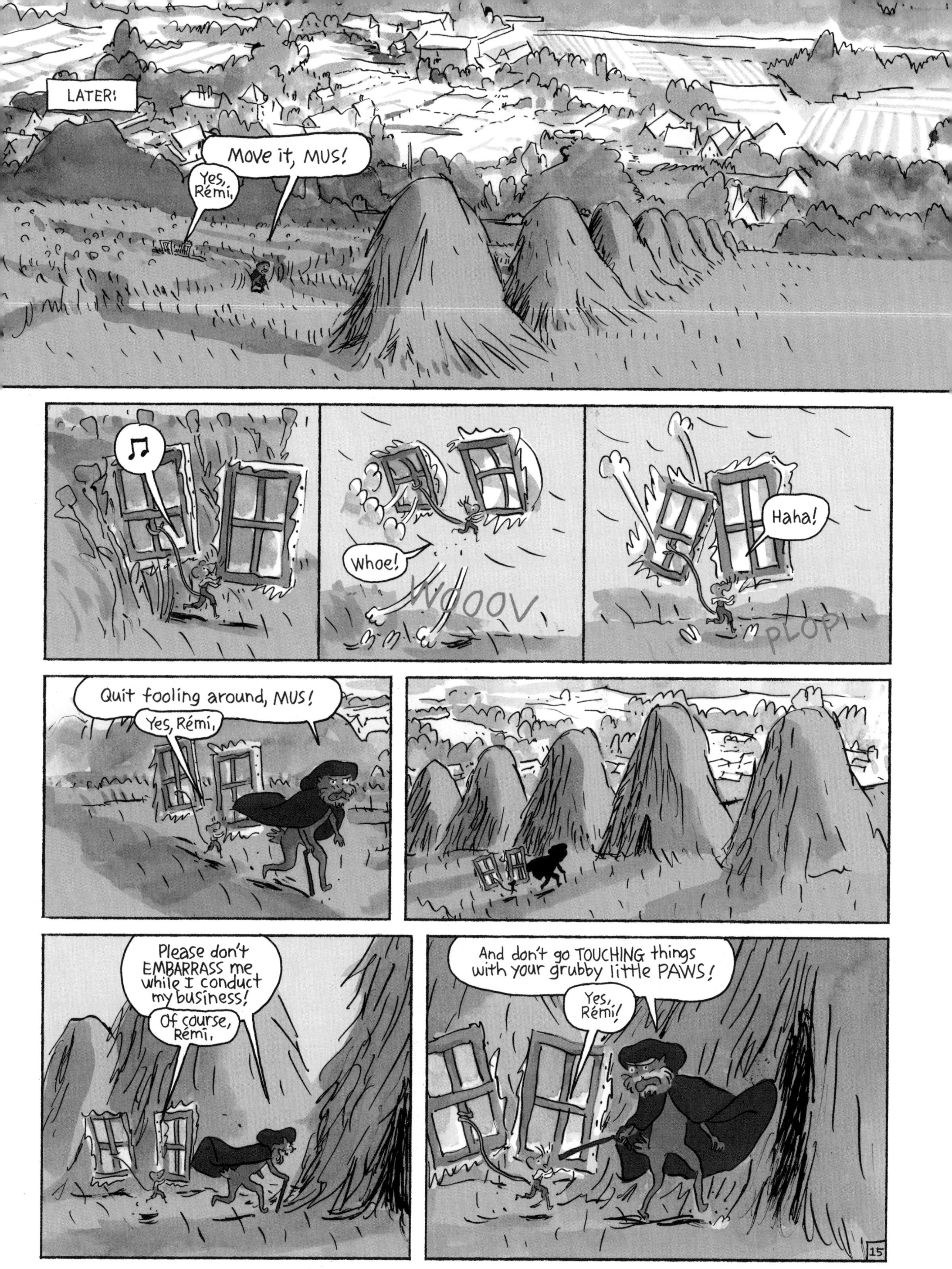
LATER:
Move it, MUS!
Yes, Rémi.
♫
Whoe!
WOOOV
Haha!
PLOP
Quit fooling around, MUS!
Yes, Rémi.
Please don't EMBARRASS me while I conduct my business!
Of course, Rémi.
And don't go TOUCHING things with your grubby little PAWS!
Yes, Rémi!
15

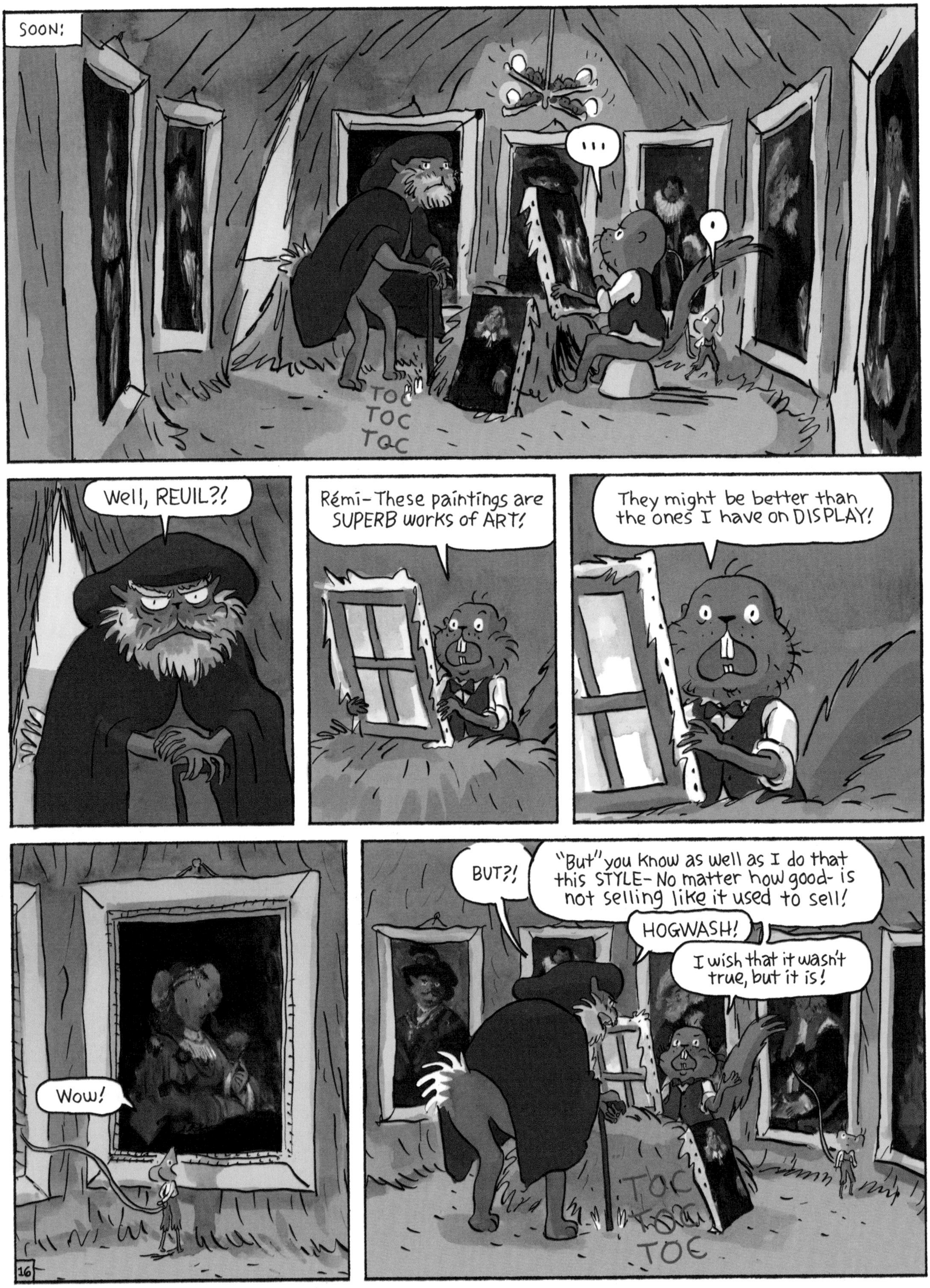
SOON:
...
!
TOC TOC TOC
Well, REUIL?!
Rémi- These paintings are SUPERB works of ART!
They might be better than the ones I have on DISPLAY!
Wow!
16
BUT?!
"But" you know as well as I do that this STYLE- No matter how good- is not selling like it used to sell!
HOGWASH!
I wish that it wasn't true, but it is!
TOC TOC TOC

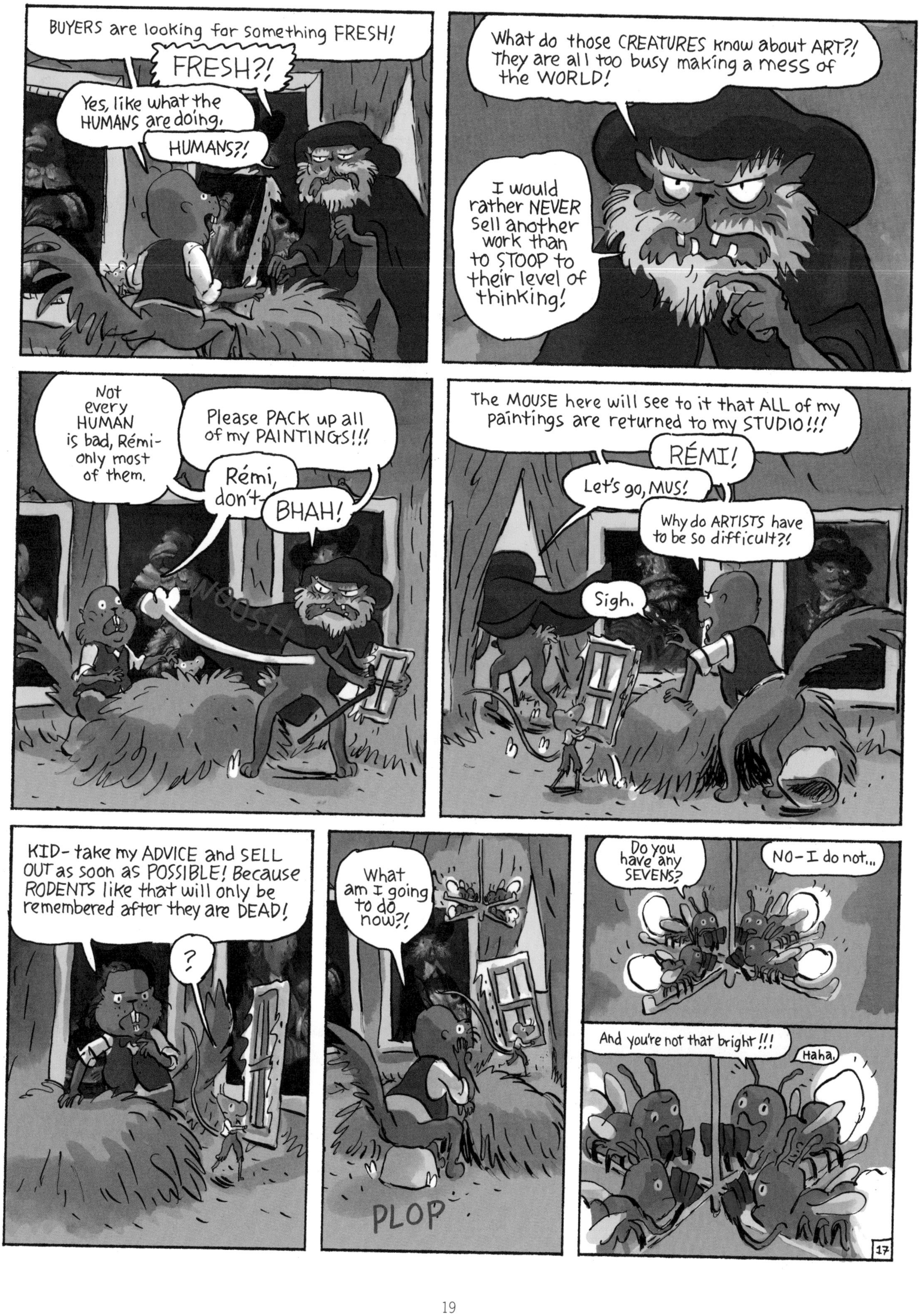
BUYERS are looking for something FRESH!
FRESH?!
Yes, like what the HUMANS are doing,
HUMANS?!
What do those CREATURES know about ART?! They are all too busy making a mess of the WORLD!
I would rather NEVER sell another work than to STOOP to their level of thinking!
Not every HUMAN is bad, Rémi- only most of them.
Please PACK up all of my PAINTINGS!!!
Rémi, don't-
BHAH!
WOOSH
The MOUSE here will see to it that ALL of my paintings are returned to my STUDIO!!!
RÉMI!
Let's go, MUS!
Why do ARTISTS have to be so difficult?!
Sigh.
KID- take my ADVICE and SELL OUT as soon as POSSIBLE! Because RODENTS like that will only be remembered after they are DEAD!
?
What am I going to do now?!
PLOP
Do you have any SEVENS?
NO- I do not...
And you're not that bright!!!
Haha.
17

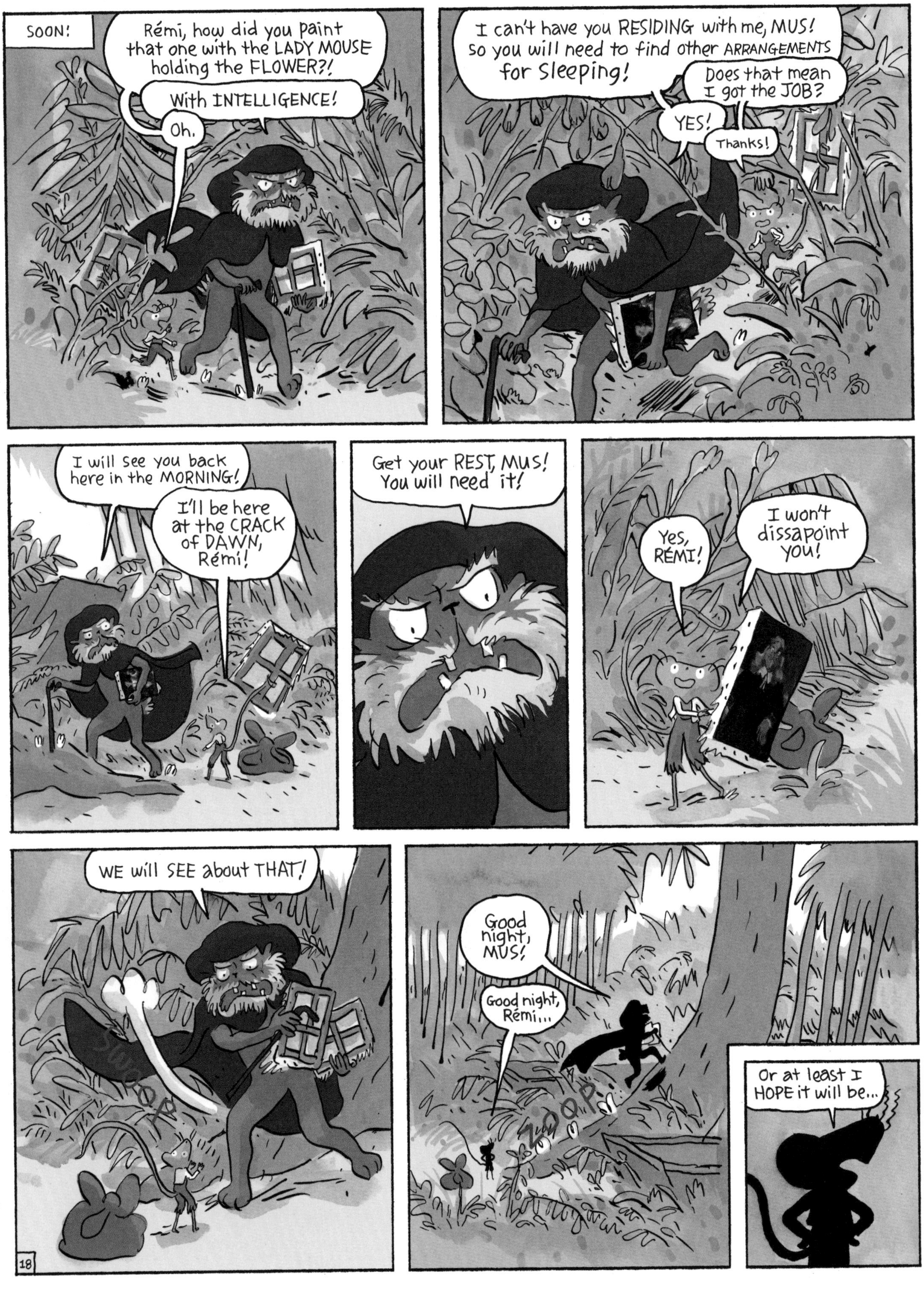
SOON!
Rémi, how did you paint that one with the LADY MOUSE holding the FLOWER?!
With INTELLIGENCE!
Oh.
I can't have you RESIDING with me, MUS! so you will need to find other ARRANGEMENTS for Sleeping!
Does that mean I got the JOB?
YES!
Thanks!
I will see you back here in the MORNING!
I'll be here at the CRACK of DAWN, Rémi!
Get your REST, MUS! You will need it!
Yes, RÉMI!
I won't dissapoint you!
WE will SEE about THAT!
SWOOP
18
Good night, MUS!
Good night, Rémi...
ZOOP
Or at least I HOPE it will be...

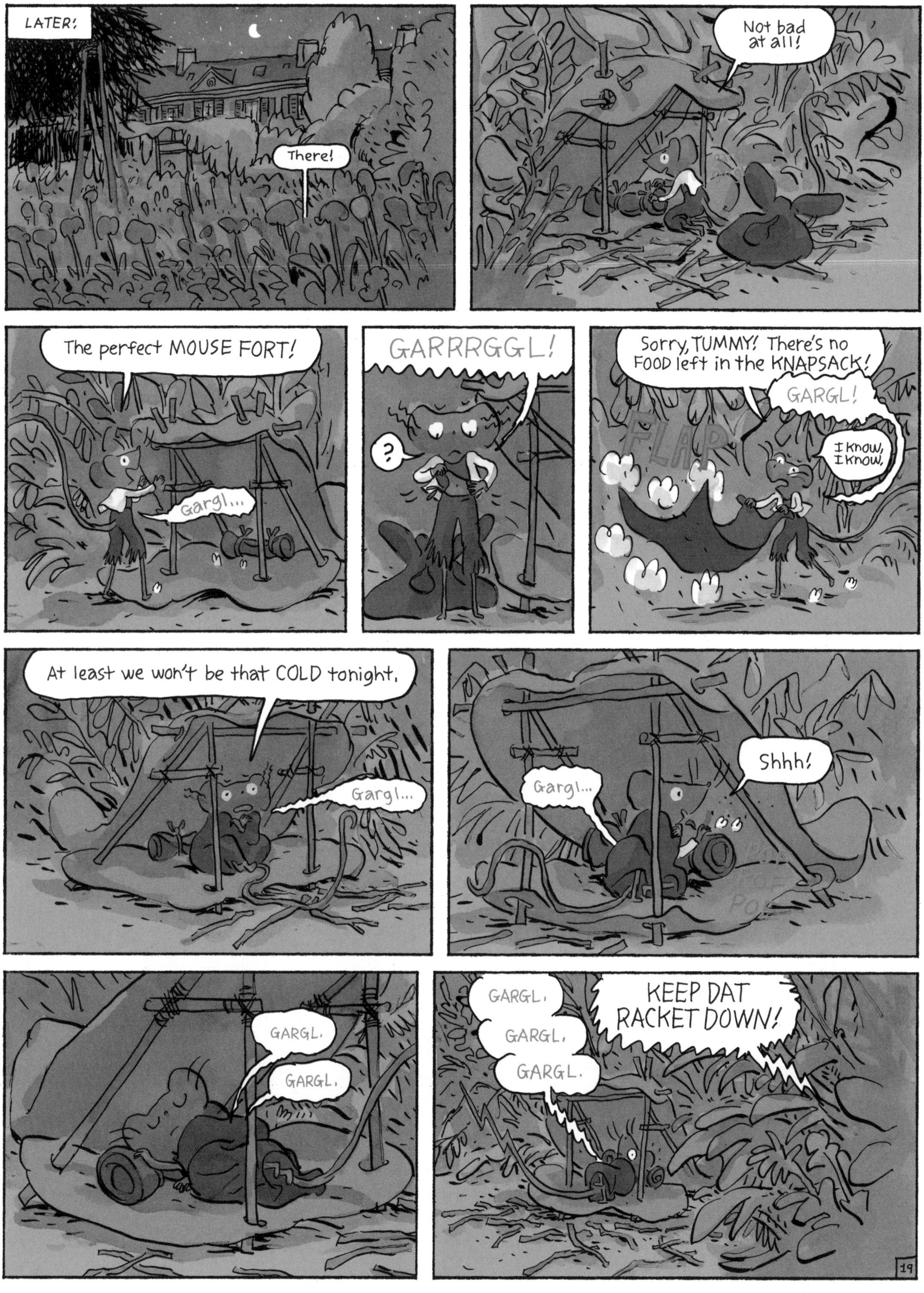
LATER:
There!
Not bad at all!
The perfect MOUSE FORT!
Gargl...
GARRRGGL!
?
Sorry, TUMMY! There's no FOOD left in the KNAPSACK!
GARGL!
FLAP
I know, I know.
At least we won't be that COLD tonight.
Gargl...
Gargl...
Shhh!
GARGL.
GARGL.
GARGL.
GARGL.
GARGL.
KEEP DAT RACKET DOWN!
19

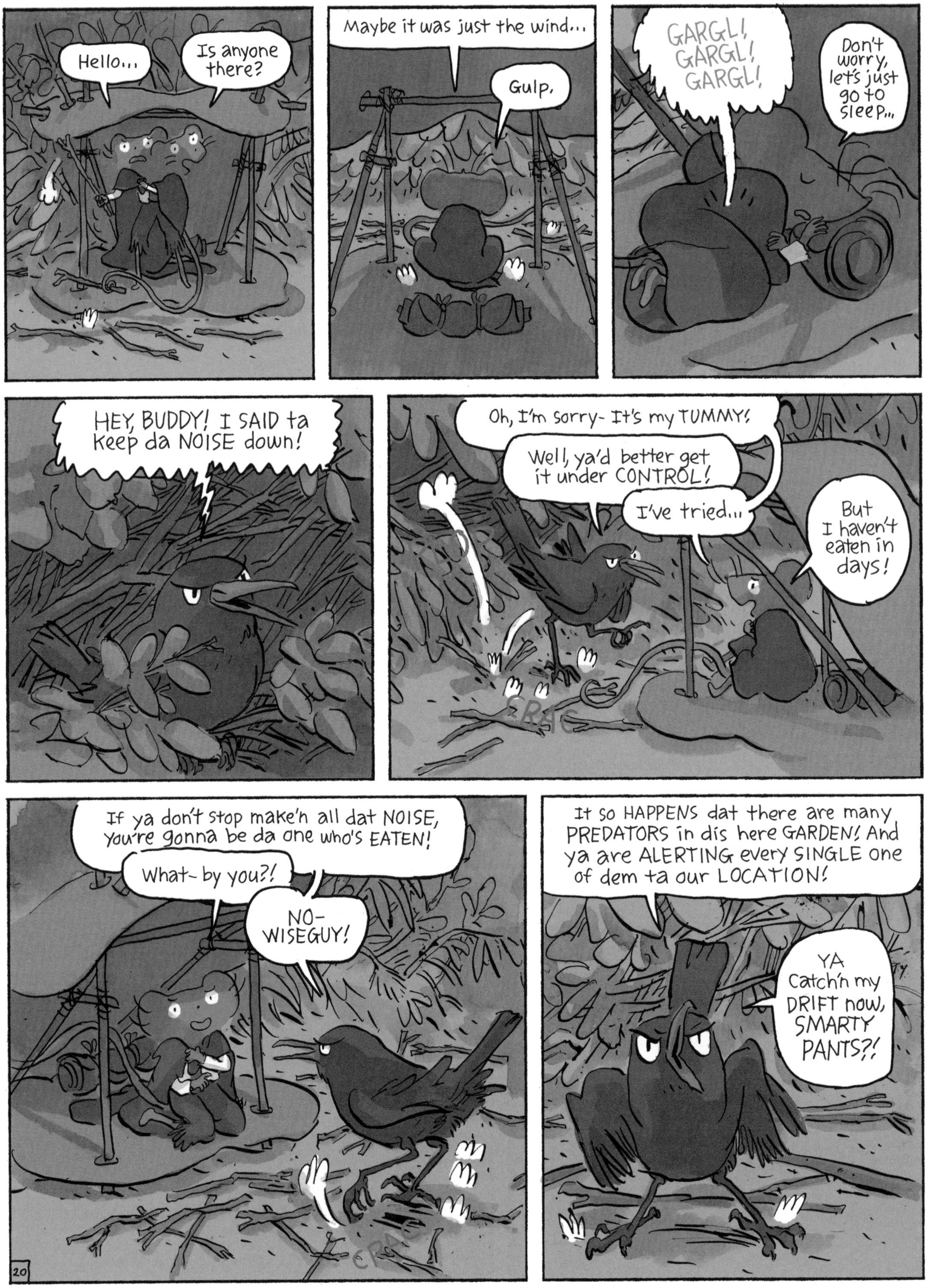

Hello...
Is anyone there?
Maybe it was just the wind...
Gulp.
GARGL! GARGL! GARGL!
Don't worry, let's just go to sleep...
HEY, BUDDY! I SAID ta keep da NOISE down!
Oh, I'm sorry- It's my TUMMY!
Well, ya'd better get it under CONTROL!
I've tried...
But I haven't eaten in days!
If ya don't stop make'n all dat NOISE, you're gonna be da one who's EATEN!
What- by you?!
NO- WISEGUY!
It so HAPPENS dat there are many PREDATORS in dis here GARDEN! And ya are ALERTING every SINGLE one of dem ta our LOCATION!
YA Catch'n my DRIFT now, SMARTY PANTS?!

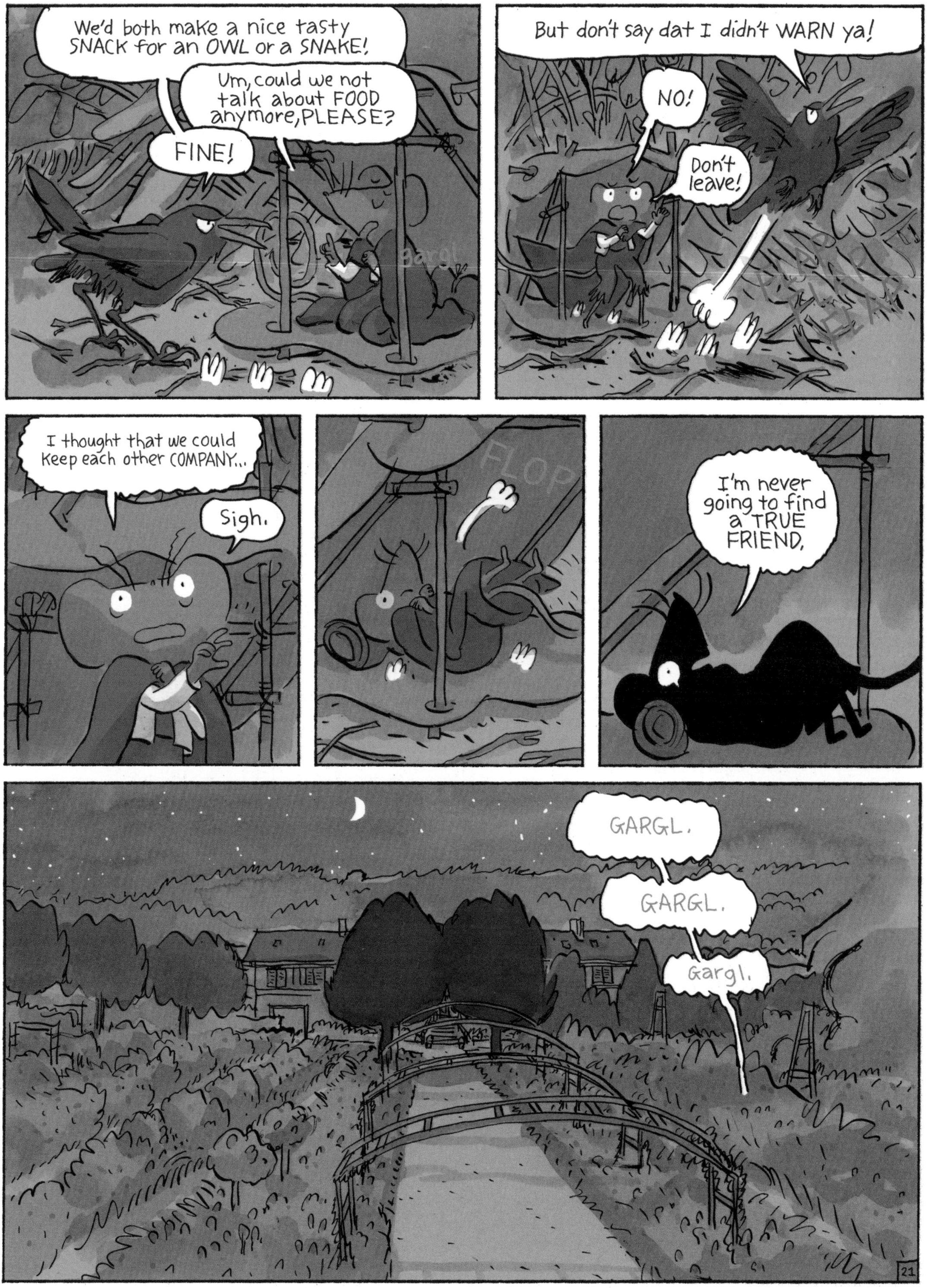
We'd both make a nice tasty SNACK for an OWL or a SNAKE!
Um, could we not talk about FOOD anymore, PLEASE?
FINE!
Gargl
But don't say dat I didn't WARN ya!
NO!
Don't leave!
I thought that we could keep each other COMPANY...
Sigh.
FLOP
I'm never going to find a TRUE FRIEND.
GARGL.
GARGL.
Gargl.
21

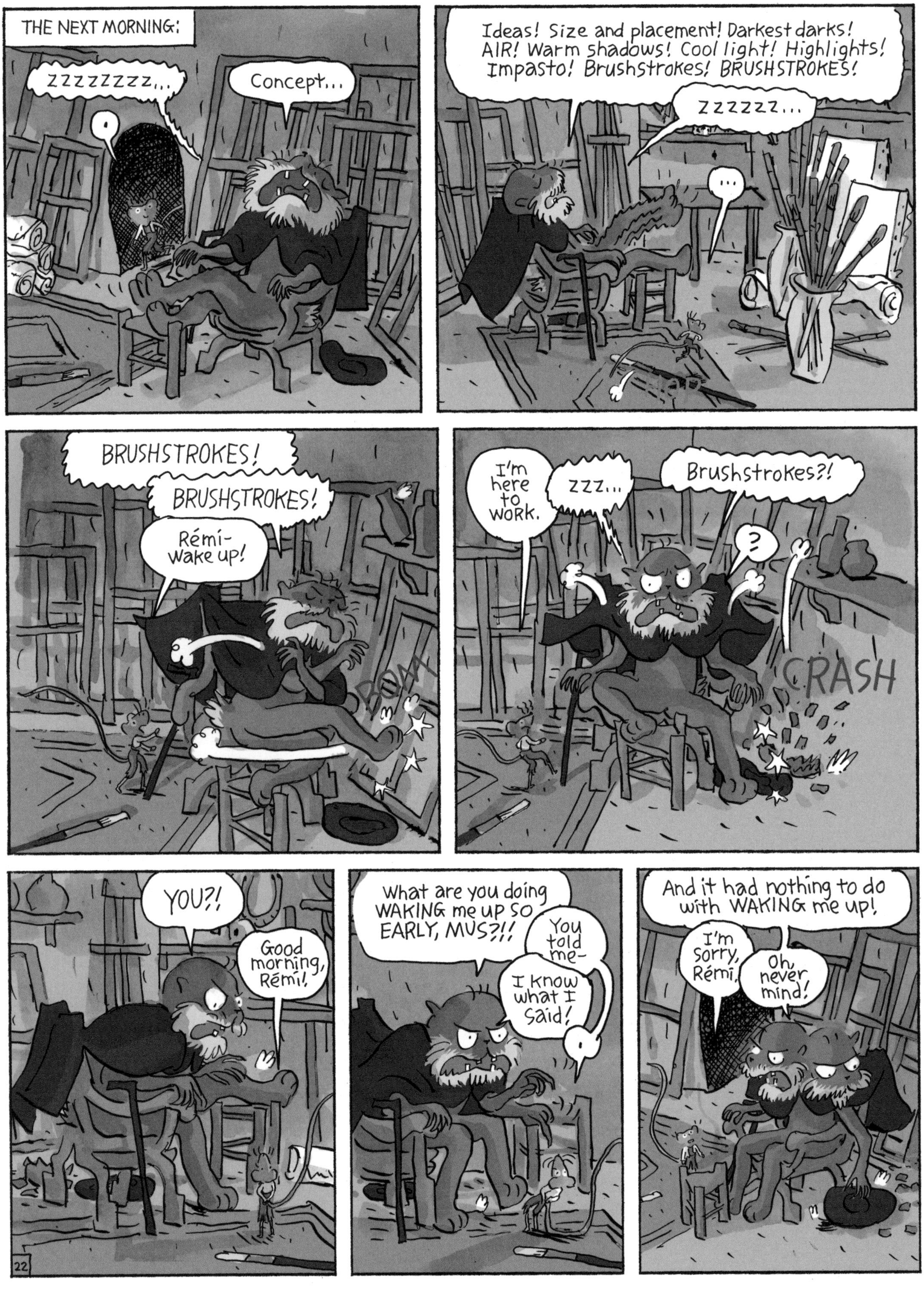
THE NEXT MORNING:
ZZZZZZZZ...
Concept...
Ideas! Size and placement! Darkest darks! AIR! Warm shadows! Cool light! Highlights! Impasto! Brushstrokes! BRUSHSTROKES!
ZZZZZZ...
...
BRUSHSTROKES!
BRUSHSTROKES!
Rémi- Wake up!
I'm here to work.
ZZZ...
Brushstrokes?!
?
CRASH
YOU?!
Good morning, Rémi!
What are you doing WAKING me up SO EARLY, MUS?!!
You told me-
I know what I said!
And it had nothing to do with WAKING me up!
I'm sorry, Rémi.
Oh, never mind!

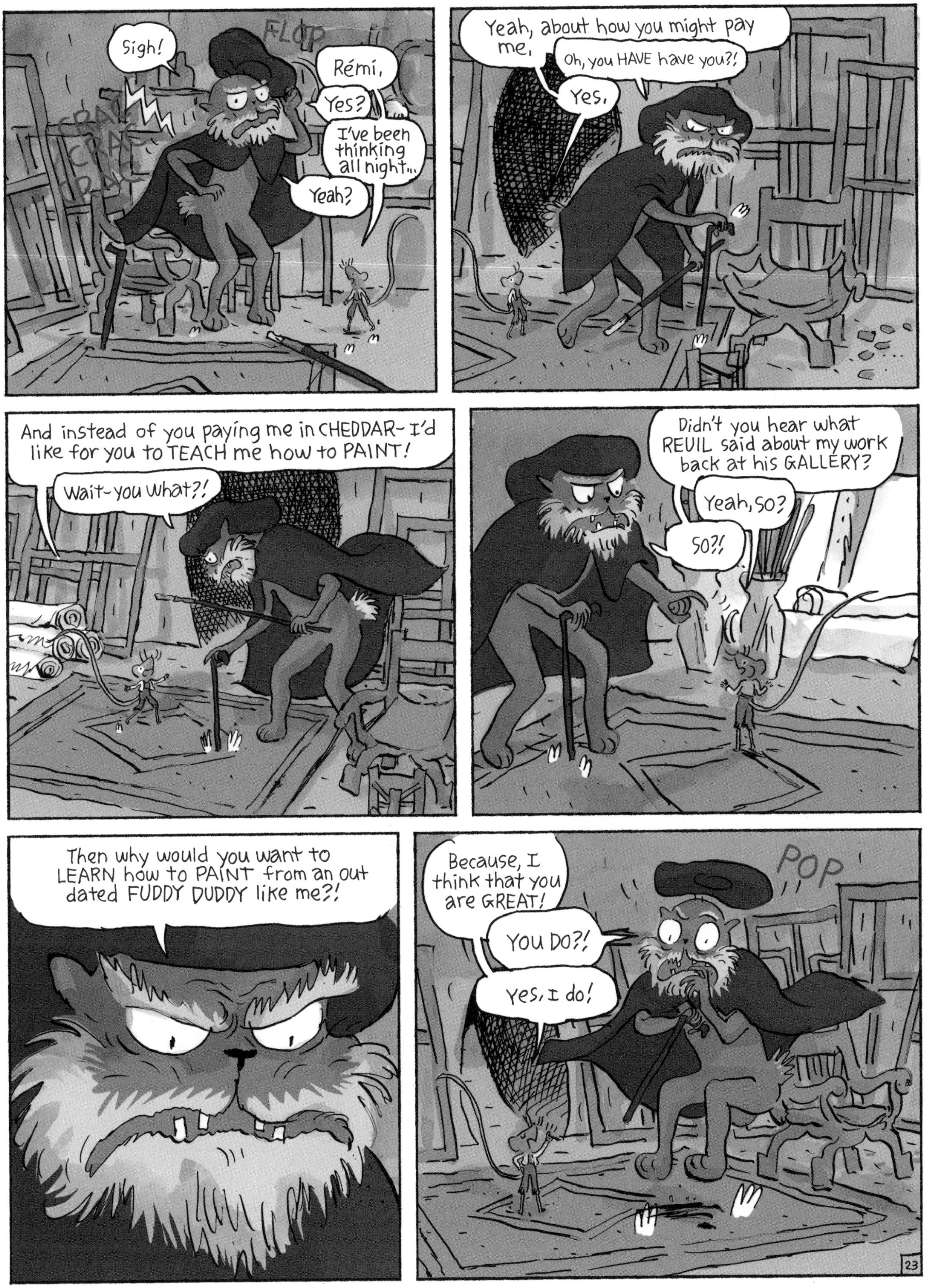
FLOP
CRAC CRAC CRAC
Sigh!
Rémi,
Yes?
I've been thinking all night...
Yeah?
Yeah, about how you might pay me,
Oh, you HAVE have you?!
Yes,
And instead of you paying me in CHEDDAR- I'd like for you to TEACH me how to PAINT!
Wait- you What?!
Didn't you hear what REUIL said about my work back at his GALLERY?
Yeah, so?
SO?!
Then why would you want to LEARN how to PAINT from an out dated FUDDY DUDDY like me?!
POP
Because, I think that you are GREAT!
YOU DO?!
Yes, I do!
23

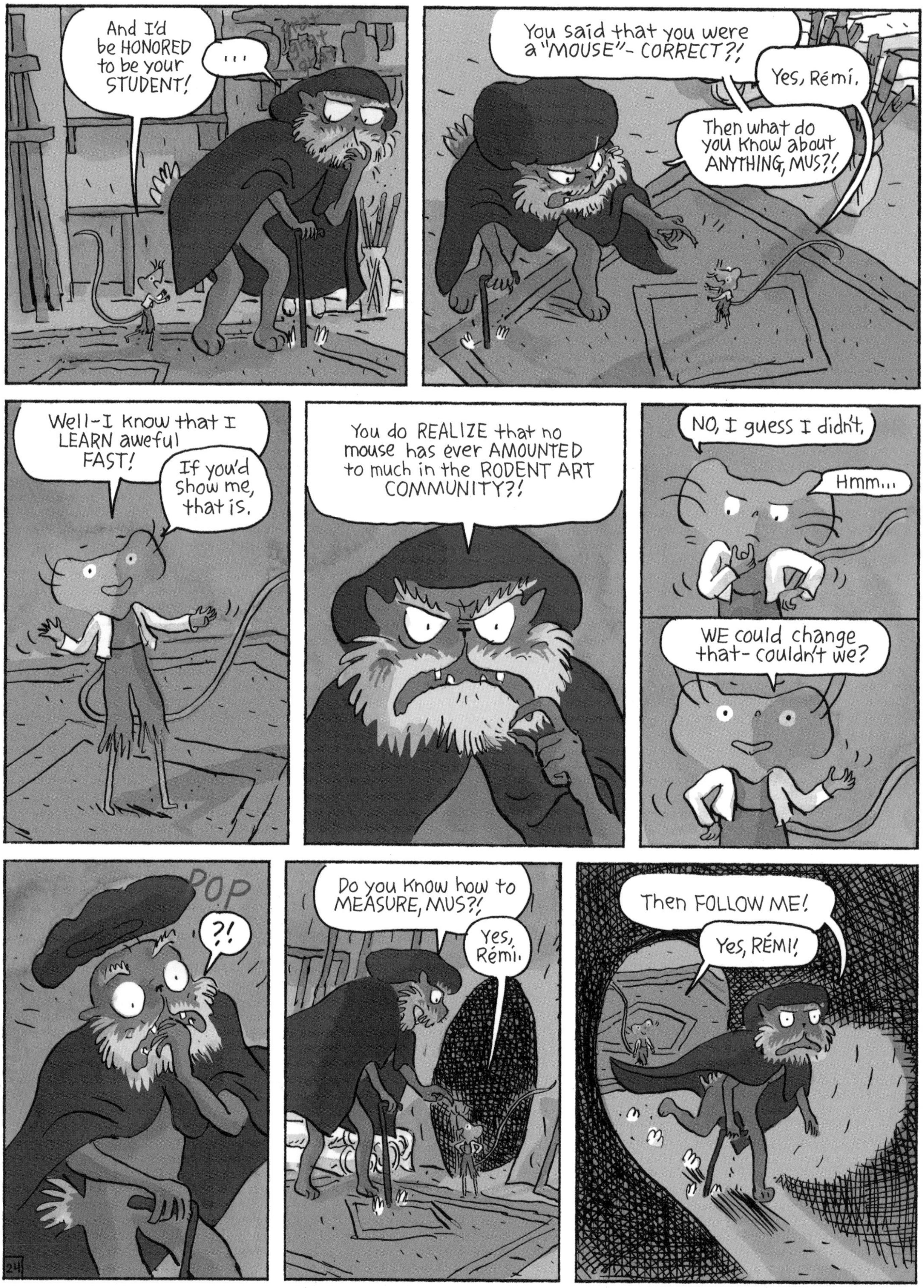
And I'd be HONORED to be your STUDENT!
...
You said that you were a "MOUSE"- CORRECT?!
Yes, Rémi.
Then what do you know about ANYTHING, MUS?!
Well-I know that I LEARN aweful FAST!
If you'd show me, that is.
You do REALIZE that no mouse has ever AMOUNTED to much in the RODENT ART COMMUNITY?!
NO, I guess I didn't.
Hmm...
WE could change that- couldn't we?
POP
?!
Do you know how to MEASURE, MUS?!
Yes, Rémi.
Then FOLLOW ME!
Yes, RÉMI!

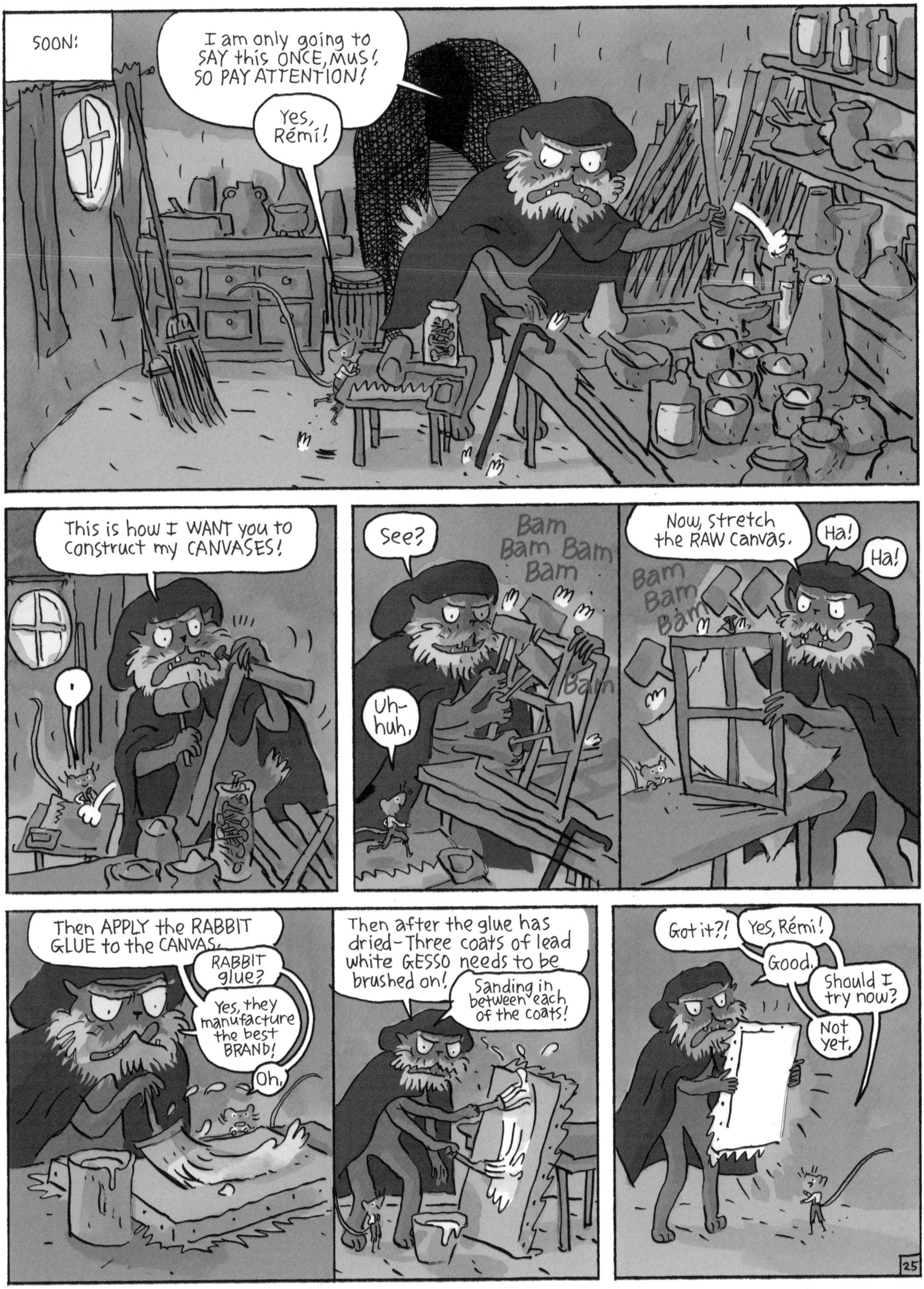

SOON:
I am only going to SAY this ONCE, MUS! SO PAY ATTENTION!
Yes, Rémi!
This is how I WANT you to construct my CANVASES!
See?
Bam Bam Bam Bam
Bam
Uh-huh.
Now, stretch the RAW canvas.
Ha!
Ha!
Bam Bam Bam
Then APPLY the RABBIT GLUE to the CANVAS.
RABBIT glue?
Yes, they manufacture the best BRAND!
Oh.
Then after the glue has dried-Three coats of lead white GESSO needs to be brushed on!
Sanding in between each of the coats!
Got it?!
Yes, Rémi!
Good.
Should I try now?
Not yet.
25

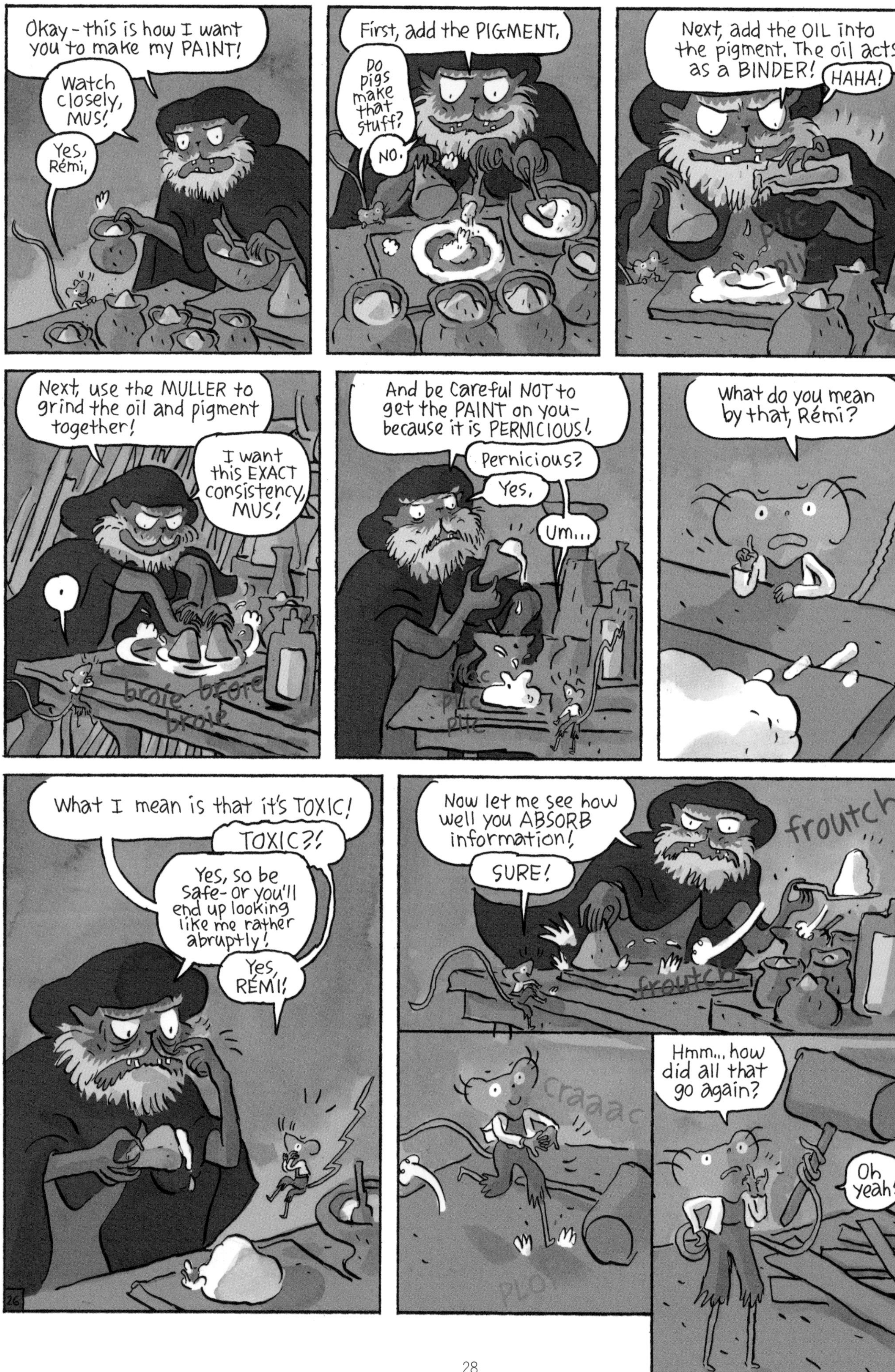
Okay - this is how I want you to make my PAINT!
Watch closely, MUS!
Yes, Rémi,
First, add the PIGMENT,
Do pigs make that stuff?
NO,
Next, add the OIL into the pigment. The oil acts as a BINDER!
HAHA!
plic
plic
Next, use the MULLER to grind the oil and pigment together!
I want this EXACT consistency, MUS!
broie
broie
broie
And be careful NOT to get the PAINT on you- because it is PERNICIOUS!
Pernicious?
Yes,
Um...
What do you mean by that, Rémi?
What I mean is that it's TOXIC!
TOXIC?!
Yes, so be safe- or you'll end up looking like me rather abruptly!
Yes, RÉMI!
Now let me see how well you ABSORB information!
SURE!
froutch
froutch
craaaac
Hmm... how did all that go again?
Oh yeah!

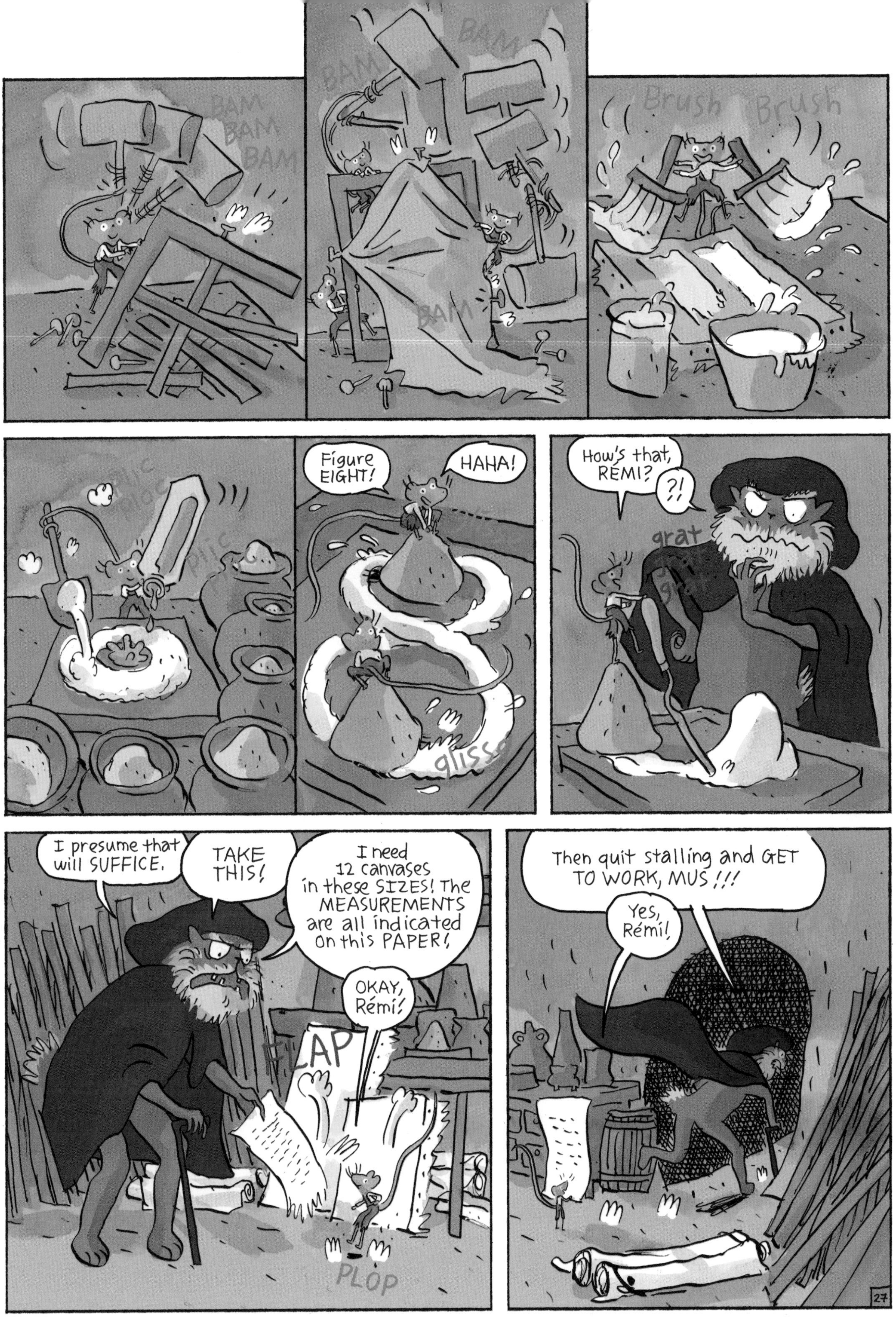
BAM
BAM
BAM
BAM
BAM
BAM
BAM
Brush
Brush
plic
ploc
plic
ploc
Figure EIGHT!
HAHA!
gliss
gliss
How's that, RÉMI?
?!
grat
grat
grat
I presume that will SUFFICE.
TAKE THIS!
I need 12 canvases in these SIZES! The MEASUREMENTS are all indicated on this PAPER!
OKAY, Rémi!
FLAP
PLOP
Then quit stalling and GET TO WORK, MUS!!!
Yes, Rémi!
27

Have you FINISHED yet, MUS?!

Yes, Rémi!

I did everything that you asked me to do!

Good! Then I will see you tomorrow morning.

But you AGREED to teach me how to PAINT!

Oh- that's RIGHT!

Go SELECT one BRUSH from my collection!

REALLY?!

Yes, really!

WOW!

Any one you PREFER!

OH BOY!

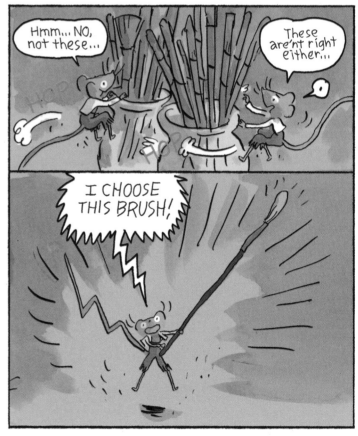

Hmm... NO, not these...

These are'nt right either...

I CHOOSE THIS BRUSH!

28

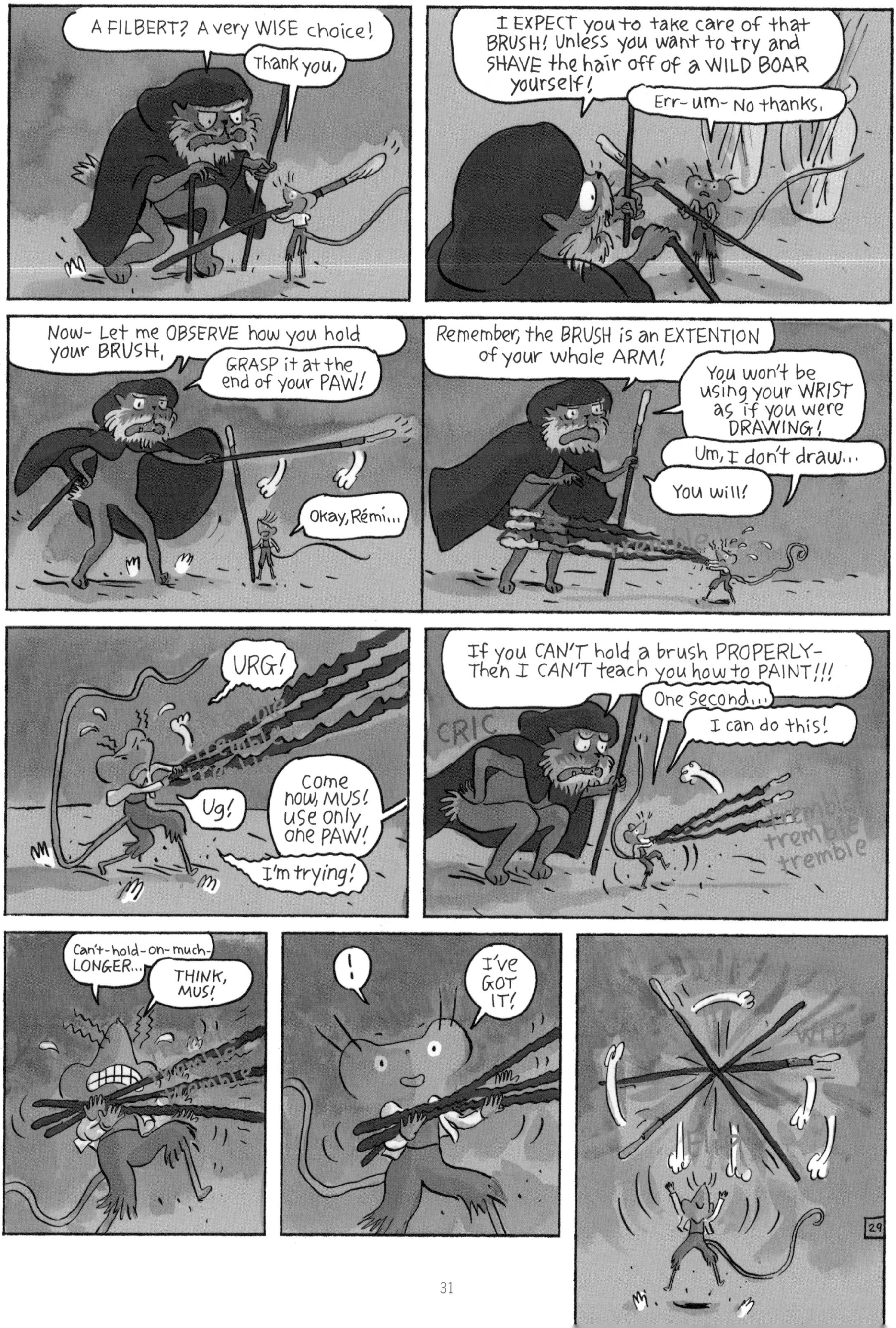

A FILBERT? A very WISE choice!
Thank you.
I EXPECT you to take care of that BRUSH! Unless you want to try and SHAVE the hair off of a WILD BOAR yourself!
Err- um- No thanks.
Now- Let me OBSERVE how you hold your BRUSH.
GRASP it at the end of your PAW!
Okay, Rémi...
Remember, the BRUSH is an EXTENTION of your whole ARM!
You won't be using your WRIST as if you were DRAWING!
Um, I don't draw...
You will!
tremble
URG!
tremble tremble
Ug!
Come now, MUS! use only one PAW!
I'm trying!
If you CAN'T hold a brush PROPERLY- Then I CAN'T teach you how to PAINT!!!
One second...
I can do this!
CRIC
tremble tremble tremble
Can't-hold-on-much-LONGER...
THINK, MUS!
tremble tremble
!
I've GOT IT!
29

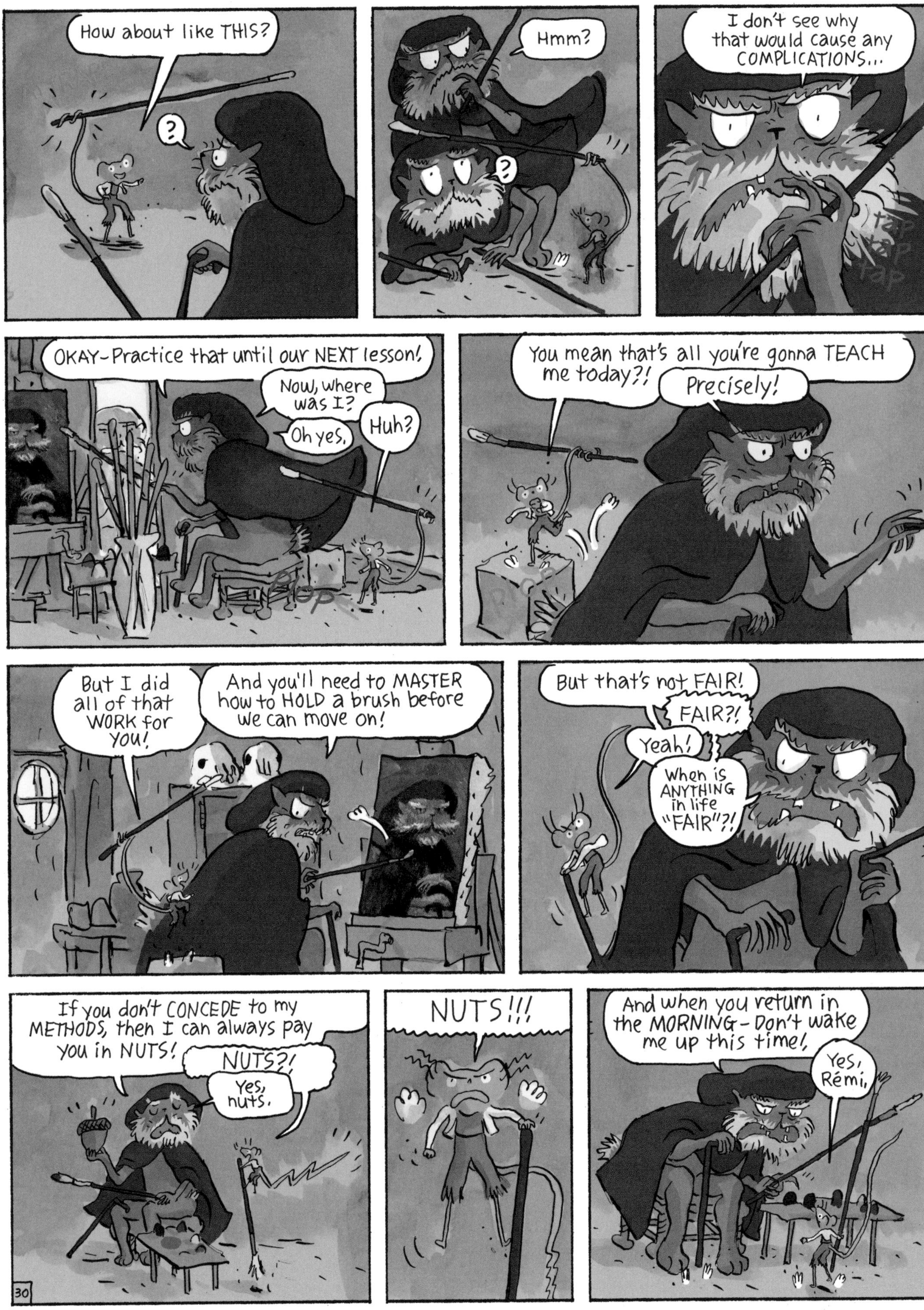
How about like THIS?
?
Hmm?
?
I don't see why that would cause any COMPLICATIONS...
tap tap tap
OKAY- Practice that until our NEXT lesson!
Now, where was I?
Oh yes.
Huh?
You mean that's all you're gonna TEACH me today?!
Precisely!
But I did all of that WORK for you!
And you'll need to MASTER how to HOLD a brush before we can move on!
But that's not FAIR!
FAIR?!
Yeah!
When is ANYTHING in life "FAIR"?!
If you don't CONCEDE to my METHODS, then I can always pay you in NUTS!
NUTS?!
Yes, nuts.
NUTS!!!
And when you return in the MORNING- Don't wake me up this time!
Yes, Rémi.

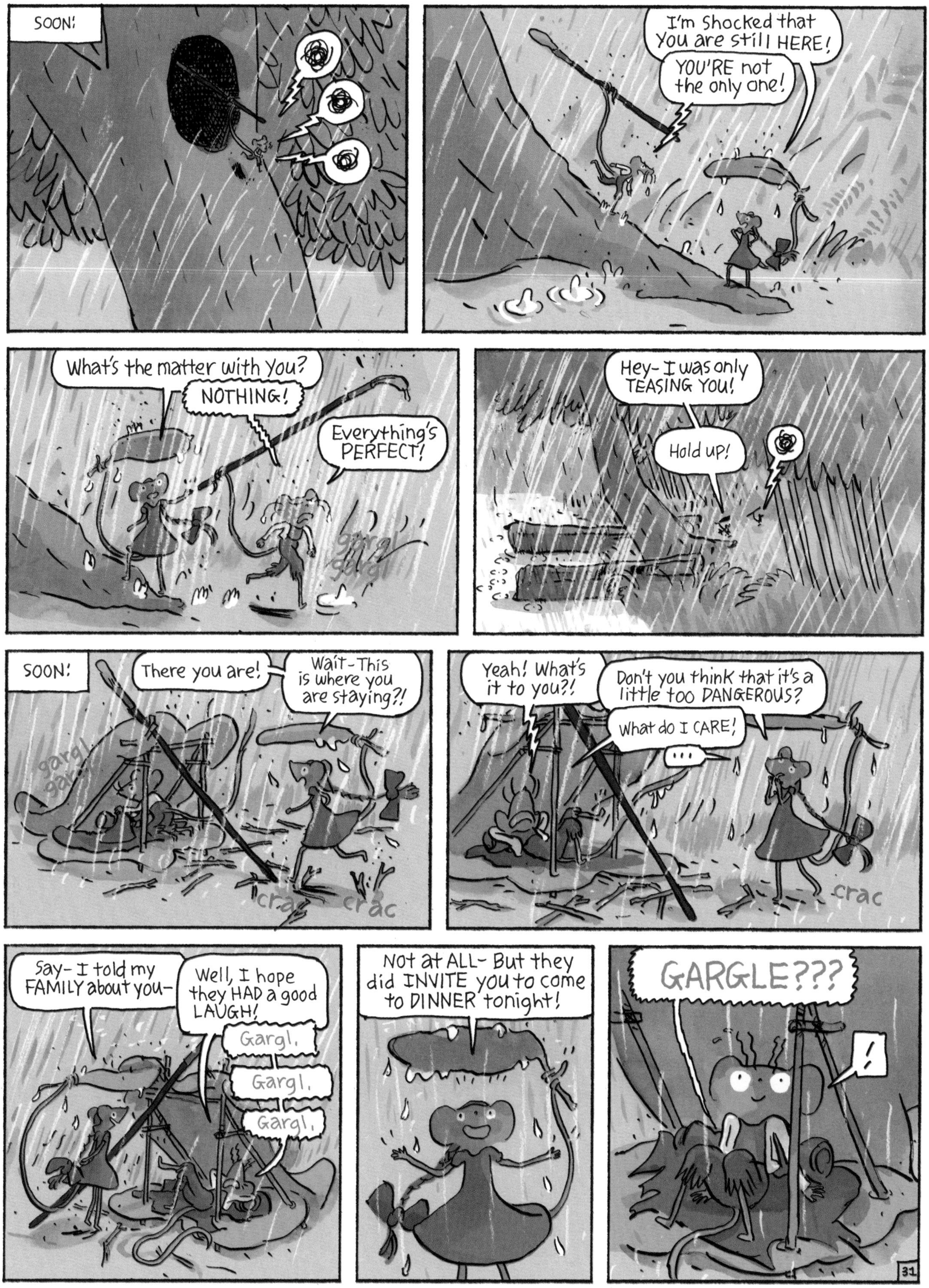
SOON:
I'm Shocked that You are still HERE!
YOU'RE not the only one!
What's the matter with you?
NOTHING!
Everything's PERFECT!
gargl
gargl
Hey- I was only TEASING YOU!
Hold up!
SOON:
There you are!
Wait- This is where you are staying?!
gargl
gargl
crac
crac
Yeah! What's it to you?!
Don't you think that it's a little too DANGEROUS?
What do I CARE!
...
crac
Say- I told my FAMILY about you-
Well, I hope they HAD a good LAUGH!
Gargl.
Gargl.
Gargl.
Not at ALL- But they did INVITE you to come to DINNER tonight!
GARGLE???
!
31

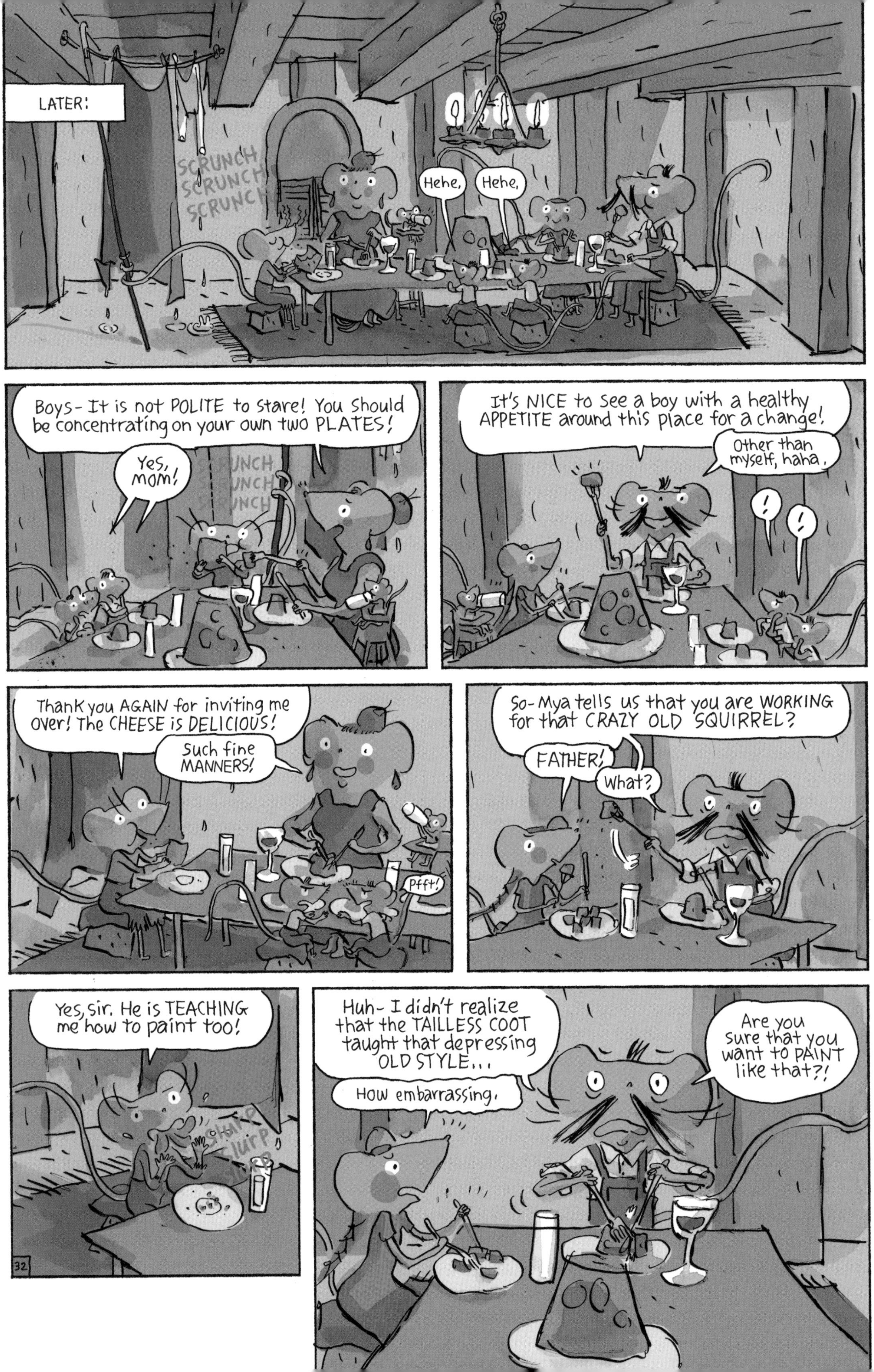
LATER:
SCRUNCH SCRUNCH SCRUNCH
Hehe,
Hehe,
Boys- It is not POLITE to stare! You should be concentrating on your own two PLATES!
Yes, mom!
SCRUNCH SCRUNCH SCRUNCH
It's NICE to see a boy with a healthy APPETITE around this place for a change!
Other than myself, haha.
!
!
Thank you AGAIN for inviting me over! The CHEESE is DELICIOUS!
Such fine MANNERS!
Pfft!
So- Mya tells us that you are WORKING for that CRAZY OLD SQUIRREL?
FATHER!
What?
Yes, Sir. He is TEACHING me how to paint too!
slurp slurp slurp
Huh- I didn't realize that the TAILLESS COOT taught that depressing OLD STYLE...
How embarrassing.
Are you sure that you want to PAINT like that?!

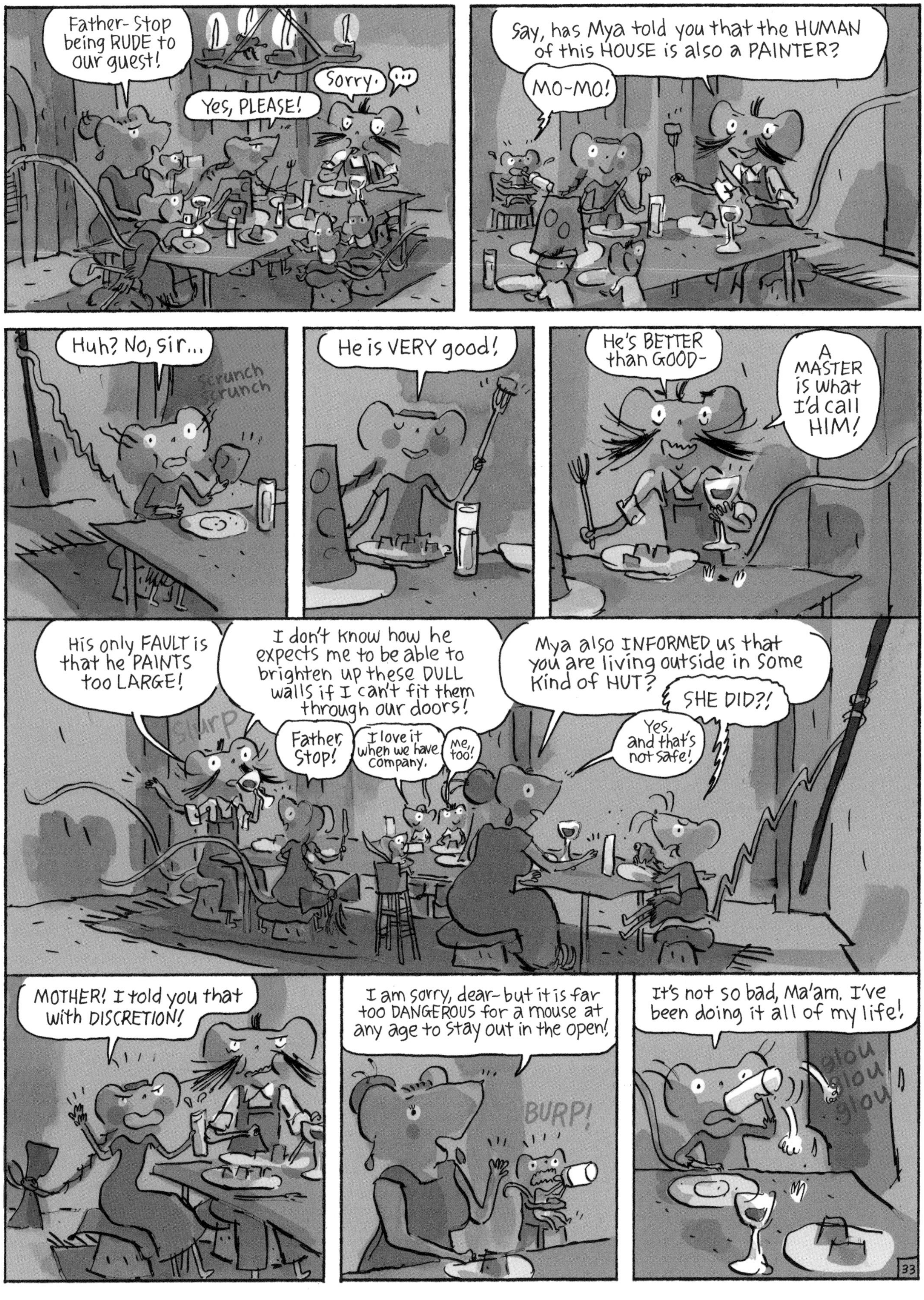

Father- Stop being RUDE to our guest!
Yes, PLEASE!
Sorry.
...
Say, has Mya told you that the HUMAN of this HOUSE is also a PAINTER?
MO-MO!
Huh? No, sir...
Scrunch scrunch
He is VERY good!
He's BETTER than GOOD-
A MASTER is what I'd call HIM!
His only FAULT is that he PAINTS too LARGE!
I don't know how he expects me to be able to brighten up these DULL walls if I can't fit them through our doors!
Slurp
Father, Stop!
I love it when we have company.
Me, too!
Mya also INFORMED us that you are living outside in some kind of HUT?
SHE DID?!
Yes, and that's not safe!
MOTHER! I told you that with DISCRETION!
I am sorry, dear- but it is far too DANGEROUS for a mouse at any age to stay out in the open!
BURP!
It's not so bad, Ma'am. I've been doing it all of my life!
glou glou glou
33

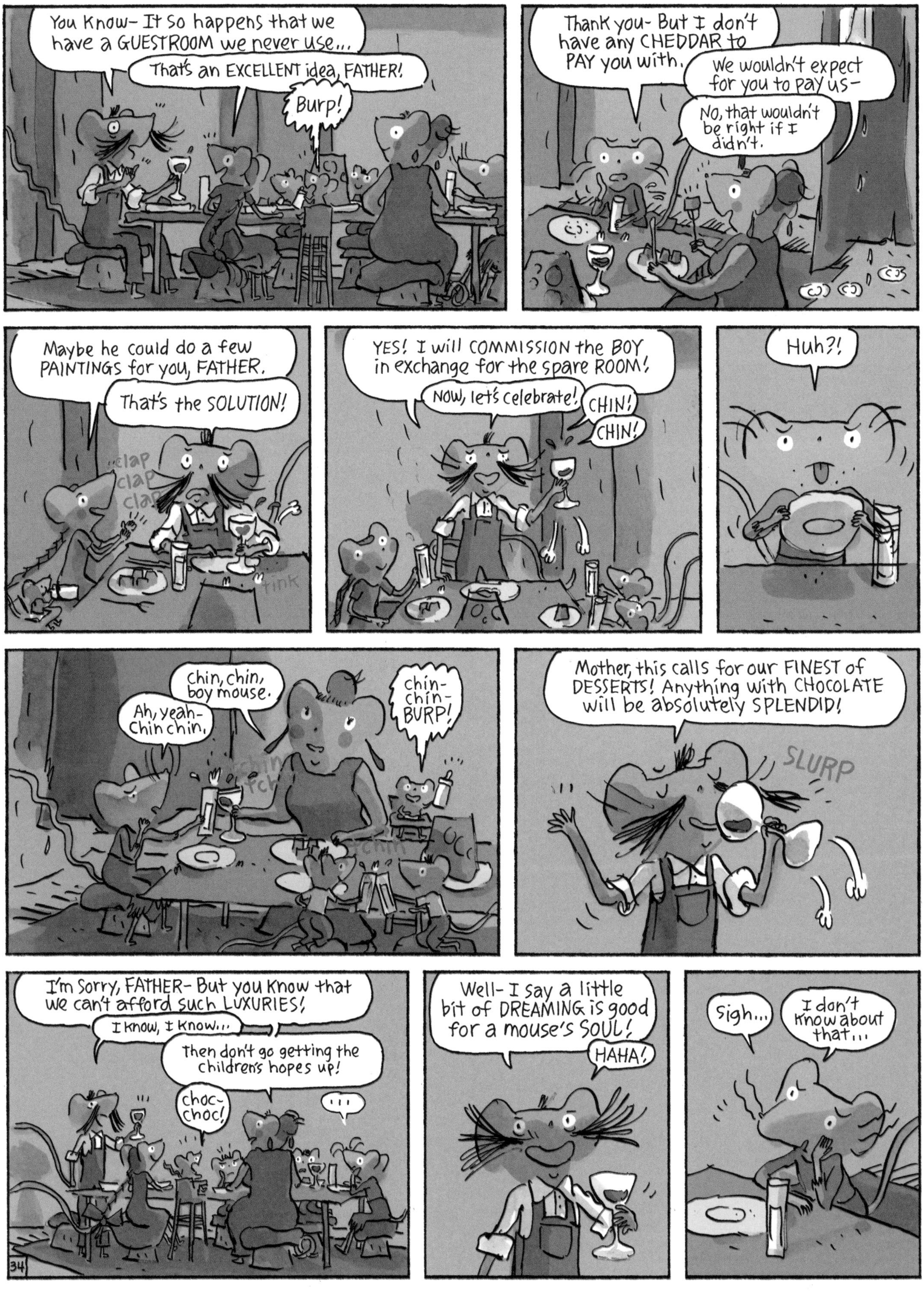
You know- It so happens that we have a GUESTROOM we never use...
That's an EXCELLENT idea, FATHER!
Burp!
Thank you- But I don't have any CHEDDAR to PAY you with.
We wouldn't expect for you to pay us-
No, that wouldn't be right if I didn't.
Maybe he could do a few PAINTINGS for you, FATHER.
That's the SOLUTION!
clap
clap
clap
tink
YES! I will COMMISSION the BOY in exchange for the spare ROOM!
Now, let's celebrate!
CHIN!
CHIN!
Huh?!
chin, chin, boy mouse.
Ah, yeah- Chin chin.
chin-chin-BURP!
Mother, this calls for our FINEST of DESSERTS! Anything with CHOCOLATE will be absolutely SPLENDID!
SLURP
I'm sorry, FATHER- But you know that we can't afford such LUXURIES!
I know, I know...
Then don't go getting the children's hopes up!
choc-choc!
...
Well- I say a little bit of DREAMING is good for a mouse's SOUL!
HAHA!
Sigh...
I don't know about that...

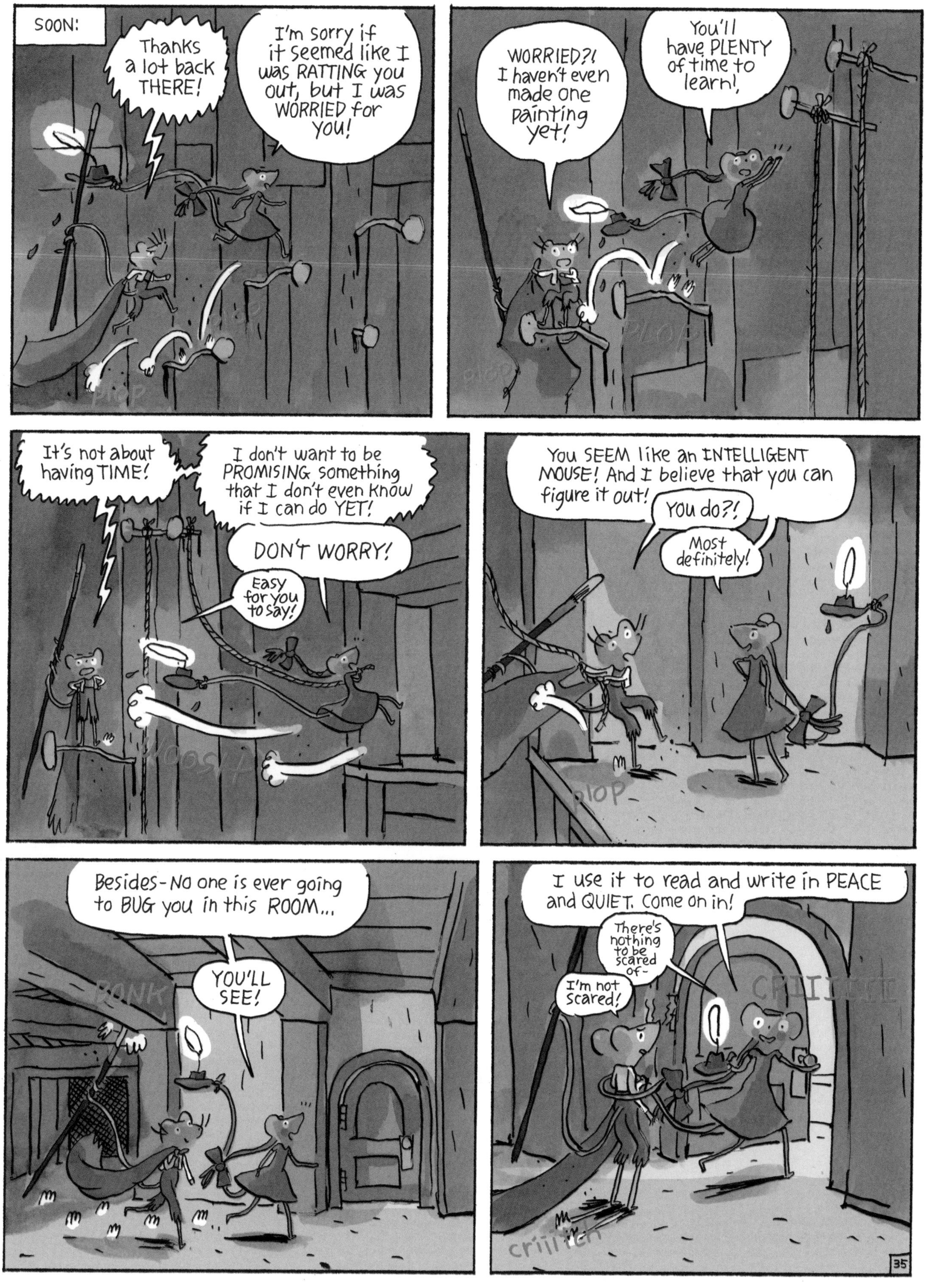

SOON:
Thanks a lot back THERE!
I'm sorry if it seemed like I was RATTING you out, but I was WORRIED for you!
plop
WORRIED?! I haven't even made one painting yet!
You'll have PLENTY of time to learn!
PLOP
It's not about having TIME!
I don't want to be PROMISING something that I don't even know if I can do YET!
DON'T WORRY!
Easy for you to say!
You SEEM like an INTELLIGENT MOUSE! And I believe that you can figure it out!
You do?!
Most definitely!
plop
Besides- No one is ever going to BUG you in this ROOM...
BONK
YOU'LL SEE!
I use it to read and write in PEACE and QUIET. Come on in!
There's nothing to be scared of-
I'm not scared!
35

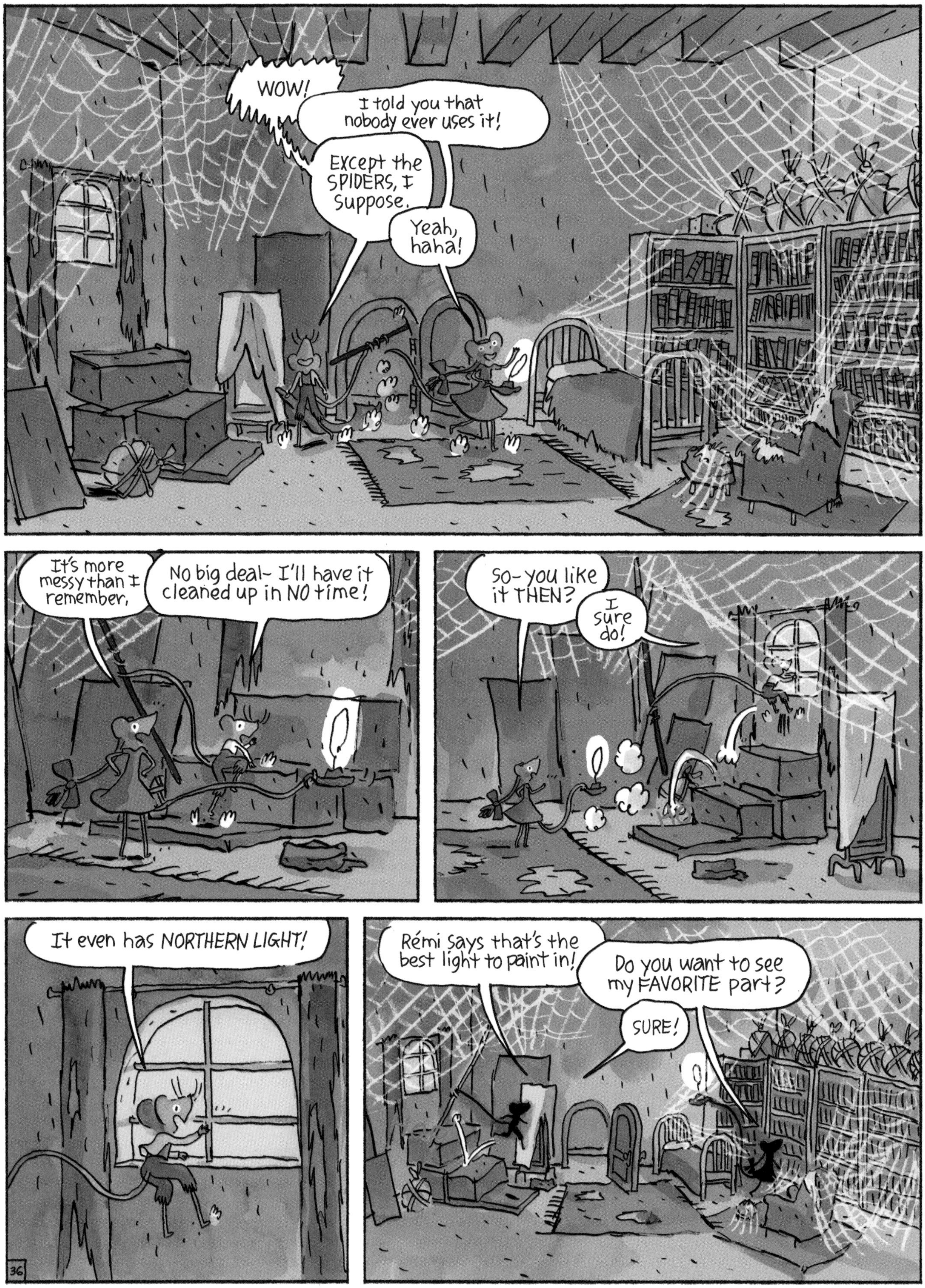
WOW!
I told you that nobody ever uses it!
Except the SPIDERS, I suppose.
Yeah, haha!
It's more messy than I remember.
No big deal- I'll have it cleaned up in NO time!
So- you like it THEN?
I sure do!
It even has NORTHERN LIGHT!
Rémi says that's the best light to paint in!
Do you want to see my FAVORITE part?
SURE!
36

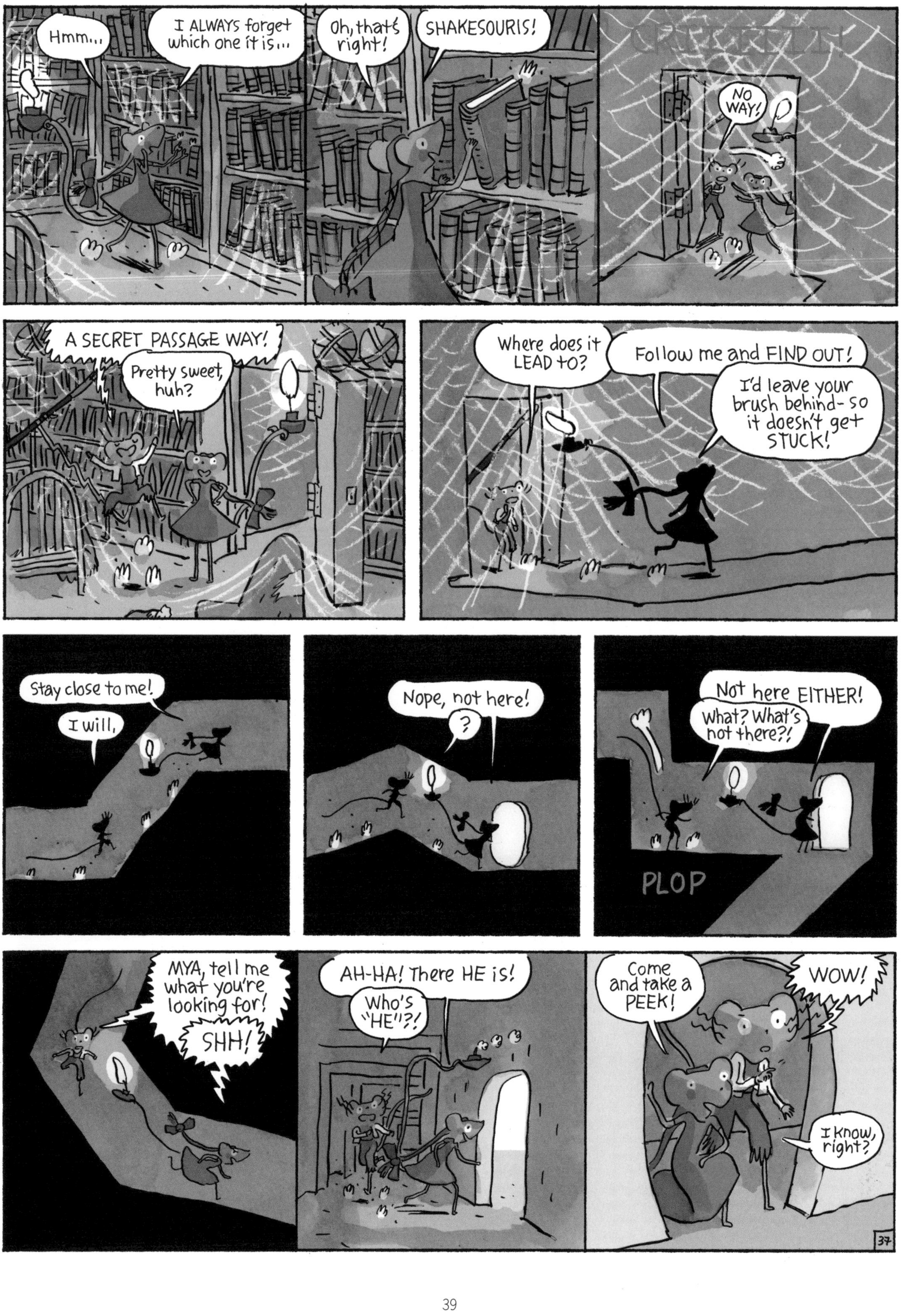
Hmm...
I ALWAYS forget which one it is...
Oh, that's right!
SHAKESOURIS!
NO WAY!
A SECRET PASSAGE WAY!
Pretty sweet, huh?
Where does it LEAD to?
Follow me and FIND OUT!
I'd leave your brush behind- so it doesn't get STUCK!
Stay close to me!
I will.
Nope, not here!
?
Not here EITHER!
What? What's not there?!
PLOP
MYA, tell me what you're looking for!
SHH!
AH-HA! There HE is!
Who's "HE"?!
Come and take a PEEK!
WOW!
I know, right?
37

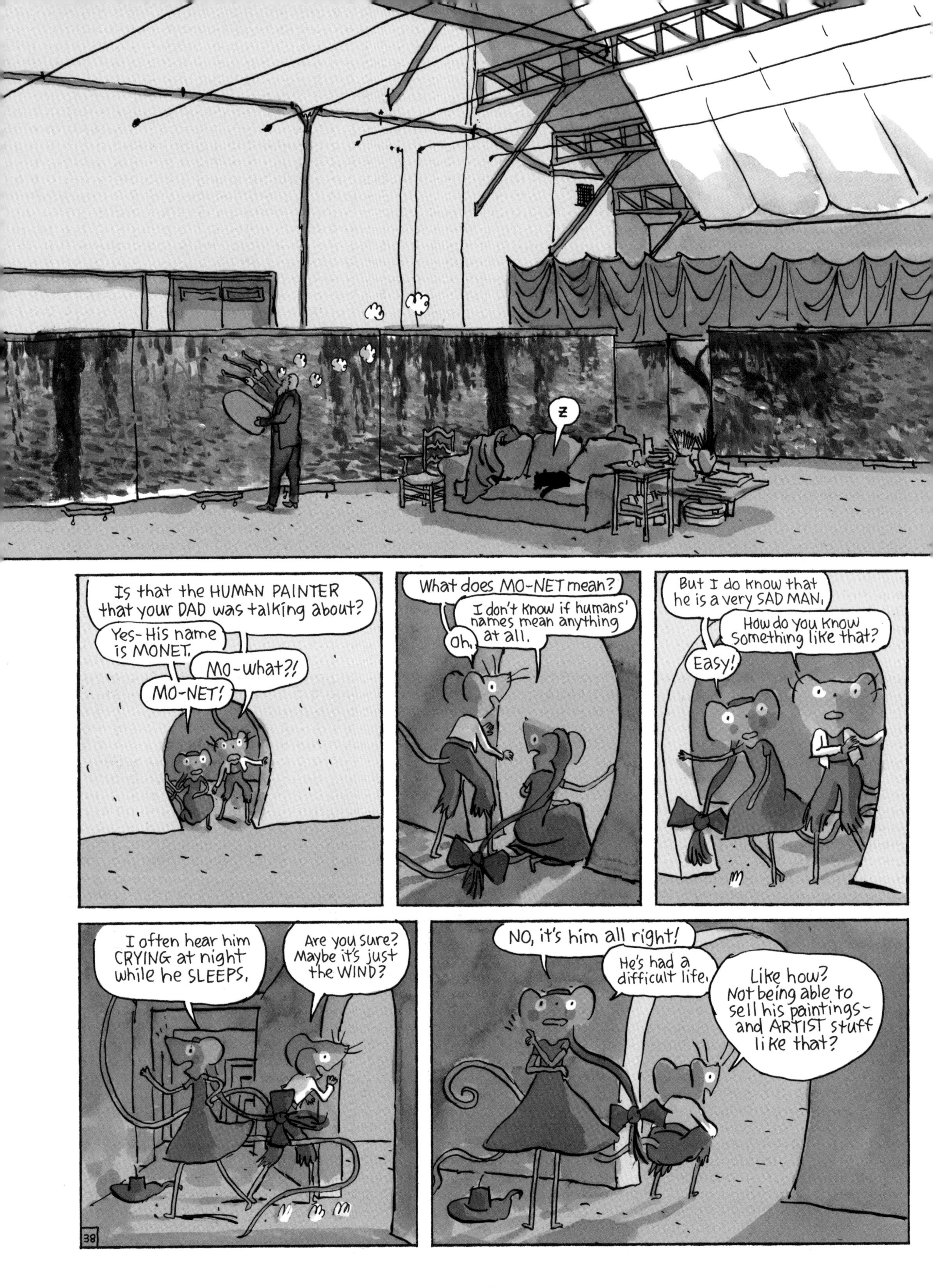

Z
Is that the HUMAN PAINTER that your DAD was talking about?
Yes- His name is MONET.
Mo-what?!
MO-NET!
What does MO-NET mean?
I don't know if humans' names mean anything at all.
Oh.
But I do know that he is a very SAD MAN.
How do you know something like that?
Easy!
I often hear him CRYING at night while he SLEEPS.
Are you sure? Maybe it's just the WIND?
38
NO, it's him all right!
He's had a difficult life.
Like how? Not being able to sell his paintings- and ARTIST stuff like that?

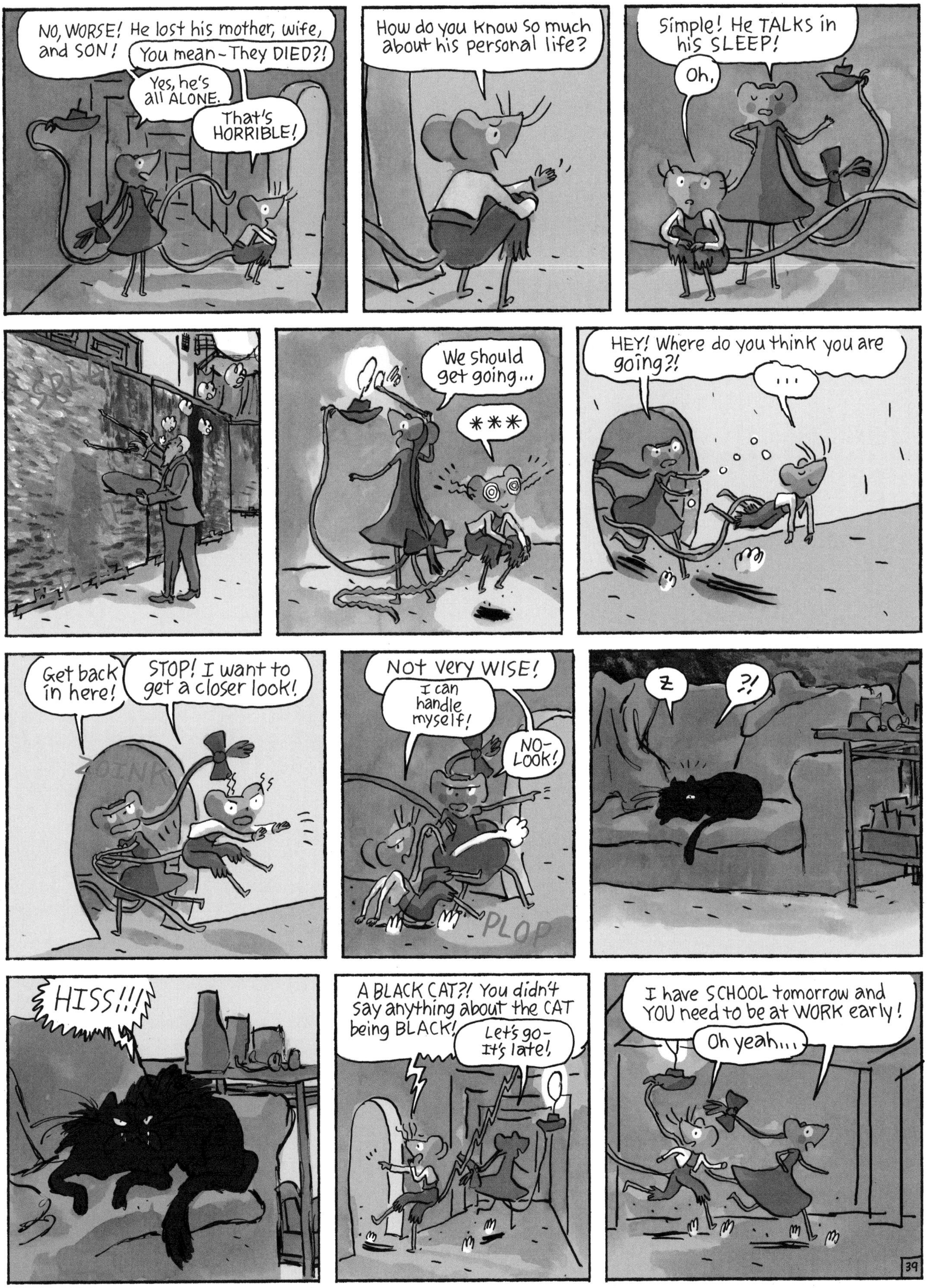
NO, WORSE! He lost his mother, wife, and SON!
You mean-They DIED?!
Yes, he's all ALONE.
That's HORRIBLE!
How do you know so much about his personal life?
Simple! He TALKS in his SLEEP!
Oh.
We should get going...
***
HEY! Where do you think you are going?!
...
Get back in here!
STOP! I want to get a closer look!
ZOINK
Not very WISE!
I can handle myself!
NO- LOOK!
PLOP
Z
?!
HISS!!!
A BLACK CAT?! You didn't say anything about the CAT being BLACK!
Let's go- It's late!
I have SCHOOL tomorrow and YOU need to be at WORK early!
Oh yeah...
39

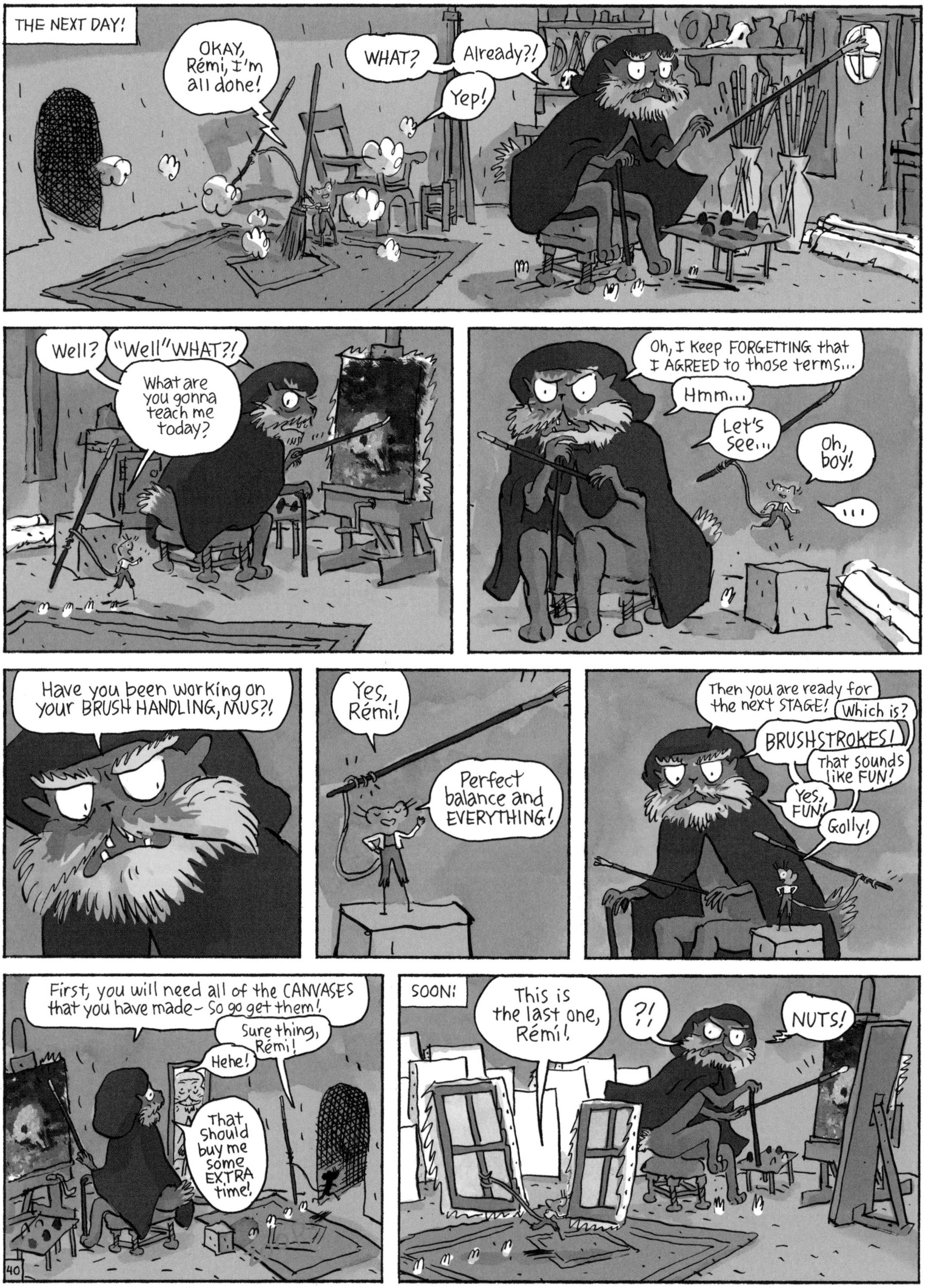
THE NEXT DAY!
OKAY, Rémi, I'm all done!
WHAT?
Already?!
Yep!
Well?
"Well" WHAT?!
What are you gonna teach me today?
Oh, I keep FORGETTING that I AGREED to those terms...
Hmm...
Let's see...
Oh, boy!
...
Have you been working on your BRUSH HANDLING, MUS?!
Yes, Rémi!
Perfect balance and EVERYTHING!
Then you are ready for the next STAGE!
Which is?
BRUSHSTROKES!
That sounds like FUN!
Yes, FUN!
Golly!
First, you will need all of the CANVASES that you have made - So go get them!
Sure thing, Rémi!
Hehe!
That should buy me some EXTRA time!
40
SOON!
This is the last one, Rémi!
?!
NUTS!

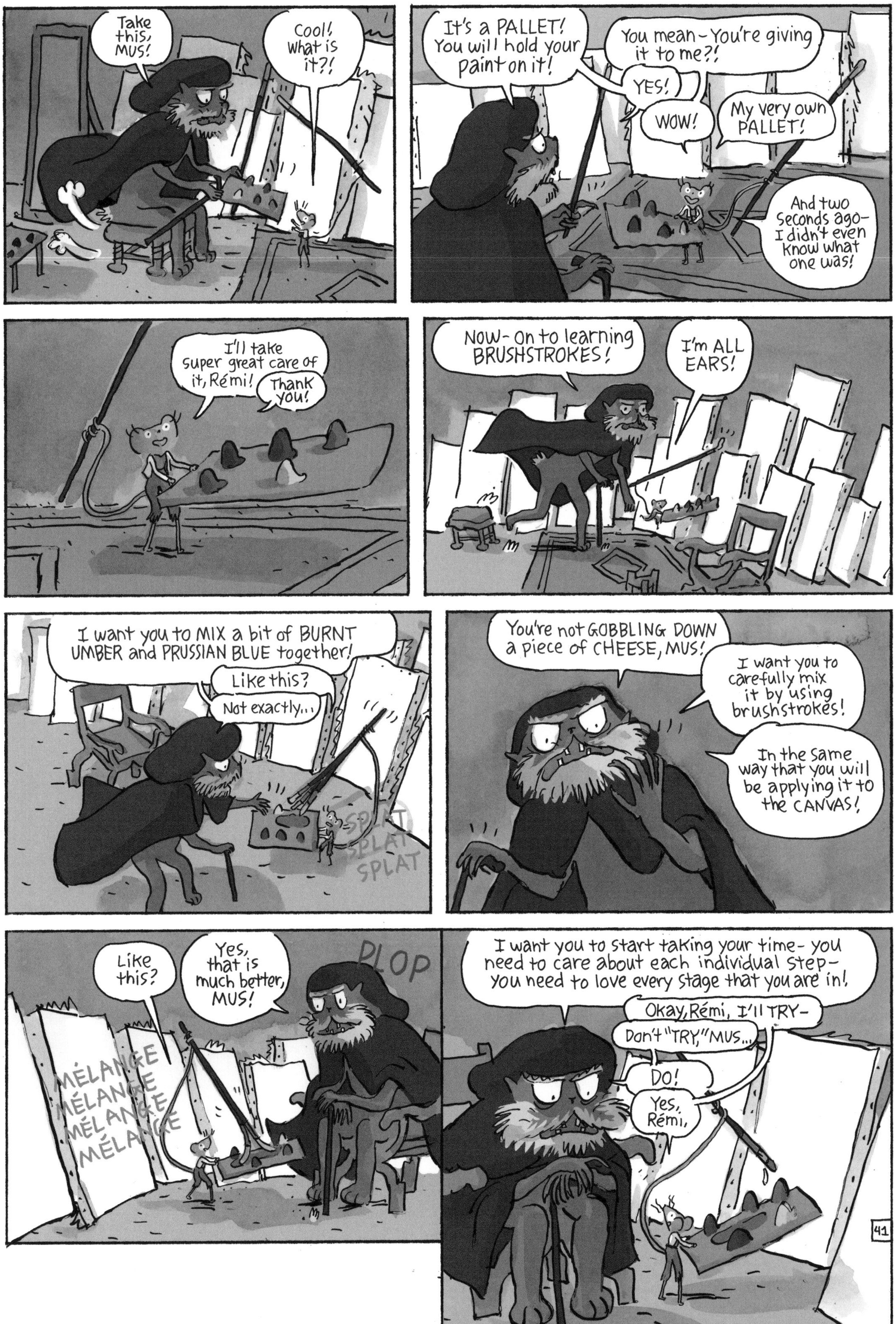
Take this, MUS!
Cool! What is it?!
It's a PALLET! You will hold your paint on it!
You mean - You're giving it to me?!
YES!
WOW!
My very own PALLET!
And two seconds ago - I didn't even know what one was!
I'll take super great care of it, Rémi!
Thank you!
NOW - On to learning BRUSHSTROKES!
I'm ALL EARS!
I want you to MIX a bit of BURNT UMBER and PRUSSIAN BLUE together!
Like this?
Not exactly...
SPLAT SPLAT SPLAT
You're not GOBBLING DOWN a piece of CHEESE, MUS!
I want you to carefully mix it by using brushstrokes!
In the same way that you will be applying it to the CANVAS!
Like this?
Yes, that is much better, MUS!
PLOP
MÉLANGE MÉLANGE MÉLANGE MÉLANGE
I want you to start taking your time - you need to care about each individual step - you need to love every stage that you are in!
Okay, Rémi, I'll TRY -
Don't "TRY," MUS...
DO!
Yes, Rémi.
41

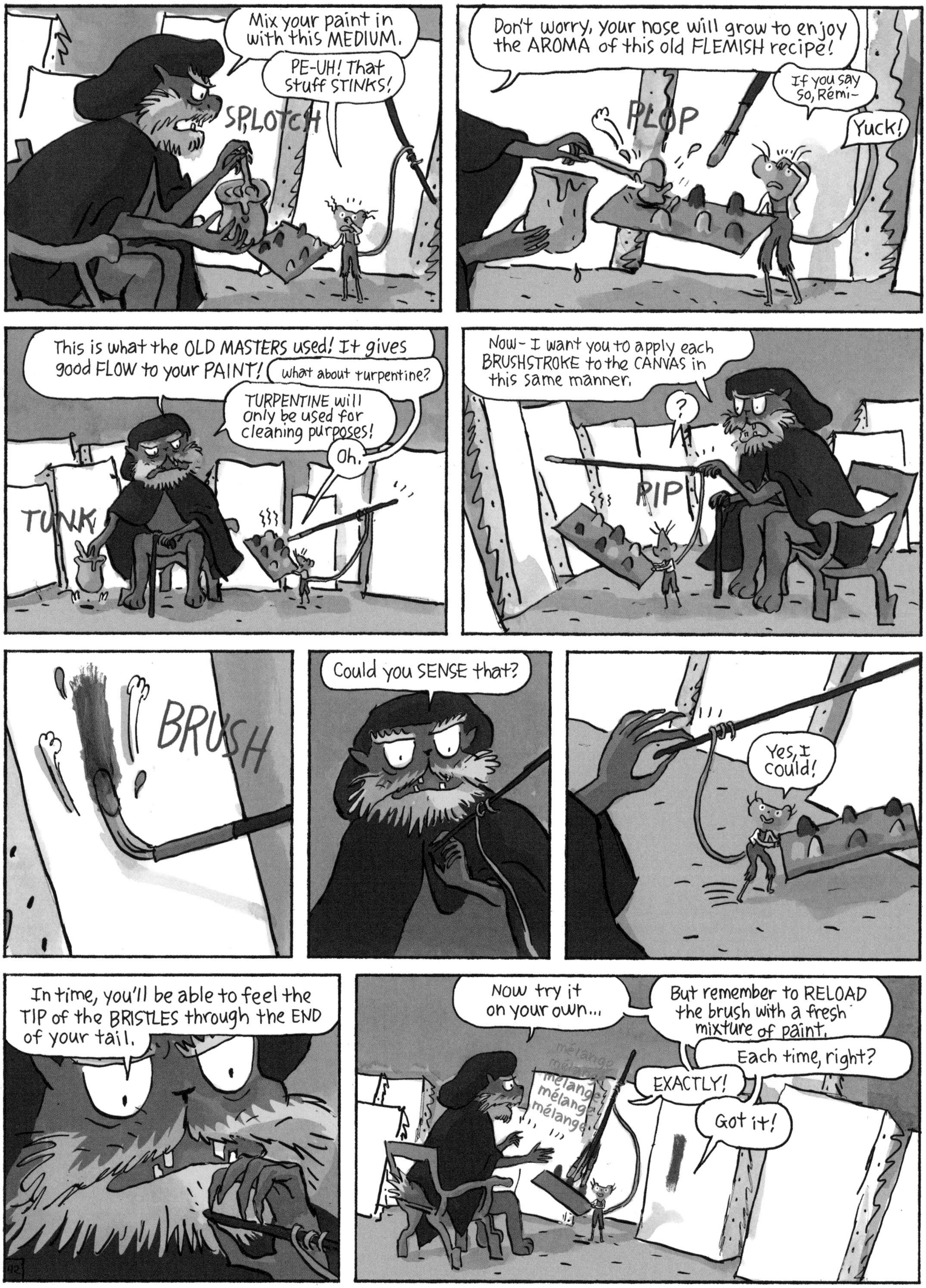

Mix your paint in with this MEDIUM.
PE-UH! That stuff STINKS!
SPLOTCH
Don't worry, your nose will grow to enjoy the AROMA of this old FLEMISH recipe!
PLOP
If you say so, Rémi-
Yuck!
This is what the OLD MASTERS used! It gives good FLOW to your PAINT!
what about turpentine?
TURPENTINE will only be used for cleaning purposes!
Oh.
TUNK
Now- I want you to apply each BRUSHSTROKE to the CANVAS in this same manner.
?
PIP
BRUSH
Could you SENSE that?
Yes, I could!
In time, you'll be able to feel the TIP of the BRISTLES through the END of your tail.
Now try it on your own...
But remember to RELOAD the brush with a fresh mixture of paint.
Each time, right?
EXACTLY!
Got it!
mélange
mélange
mélange
mélange
mélange

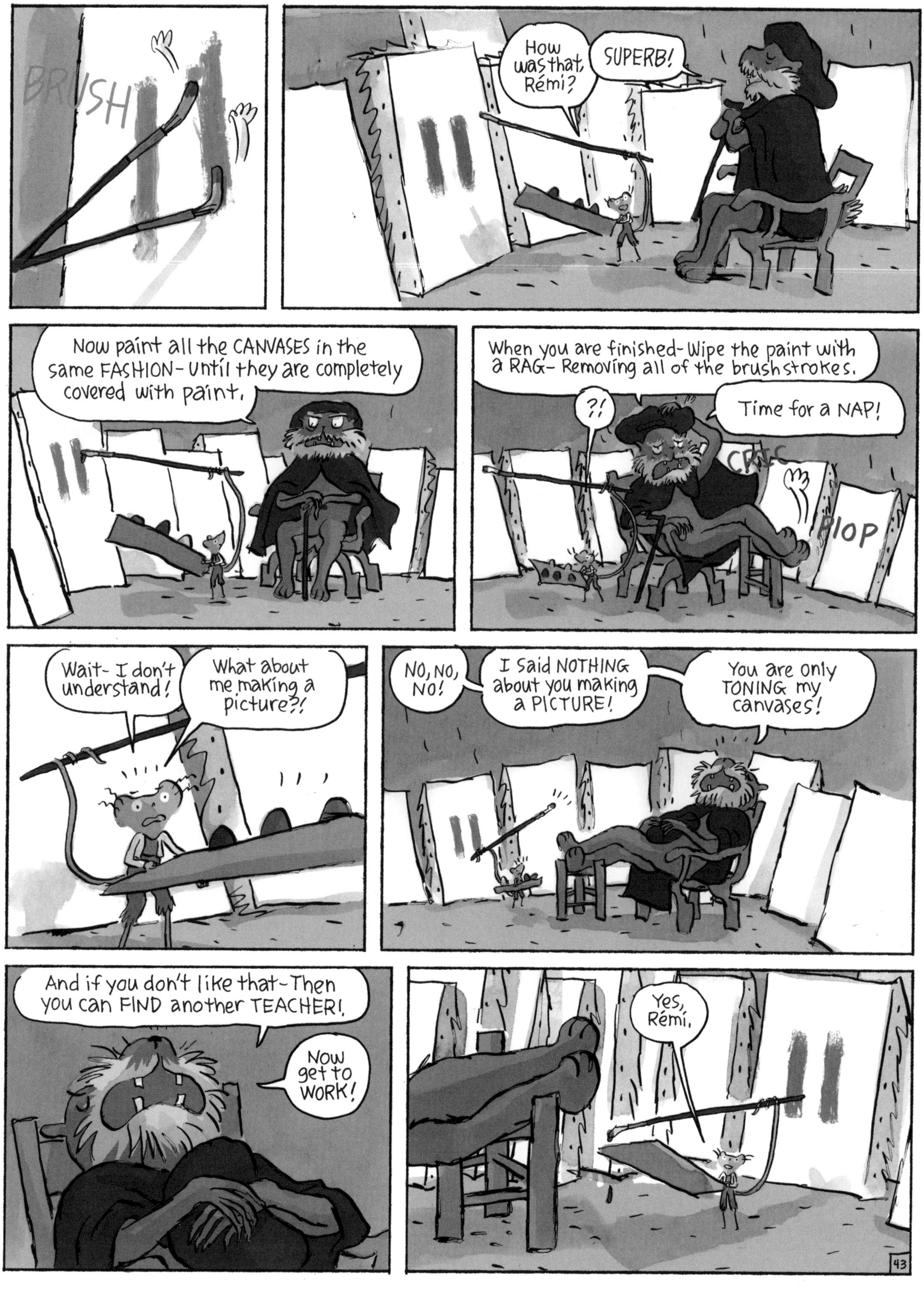
BRUSH
How was that, Rémi?
SUPERB!
Now paint all the CANVASES in the same FASHION- Until they are completely covered with paint.
When you are finished- Wipe the paint with a RAG- Removing all of the brushstrokes.
?!
Time for a NAP!
CRIC
PLOP
Wait- I don't understand!
What about me making a picture?!
NO, NO, NO!
I said NOTHING about you making a PICTURE!
You are only TONING my canvases!
And if you don't like that- Then you can FIND another TEACHER!
Now get to WORK!
Yes, Rémi.
43

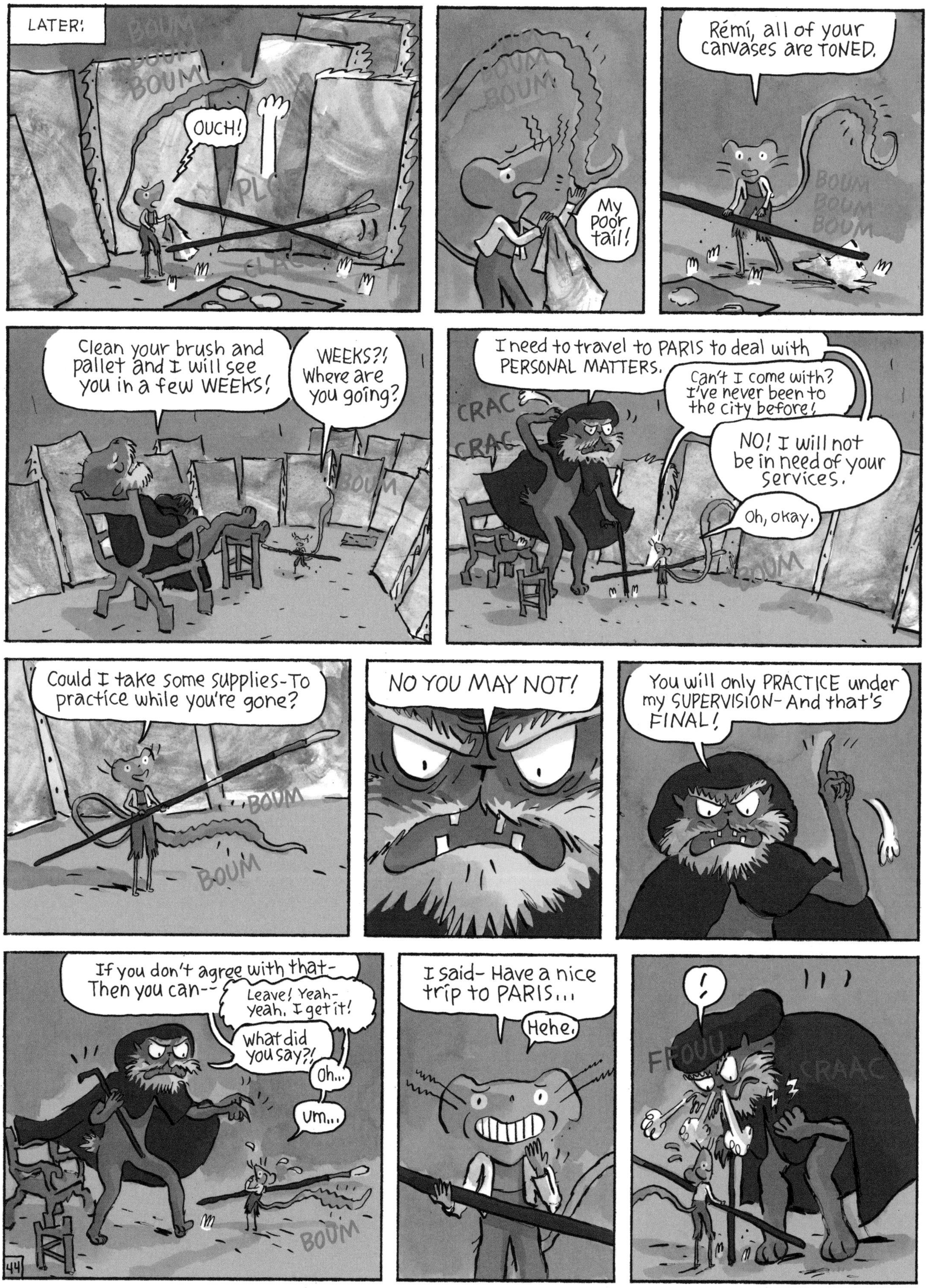

LATER!
BOUM BOUM BOUM
OUCH!
PLOC
CRAC
BOUM BOUM
My poor tail!
Rémi, all of your canvases are TONED.
BOUM BOUM BOUM
Clean your brush and pallet and I will see you in a few WEEKS!
WEEKS?! Where are you going?
BOUM
I need to travel to PARIS to deal with PERSONAL MATTERS.
CRAC
CRAC
Can't I come with? I've never been to the city before!
NO! I will not be in need of your services.
Oh, okay.
BOUM
Could I take some supplies-To practice while you're gone?
BOUM
BOUM
NO YOU MAY NOT!
You will only PRACTICE under my SUPERVISION- And that's FINAL!
If you don't agree with that- Then you can--
Leave! Yeah-yeah. I get it!
What did you say?!
Oh...
Um...
BOUM
44
I said- Have a nice trip to PARIS...
Hehe.
!
FFOUU
CRAAC

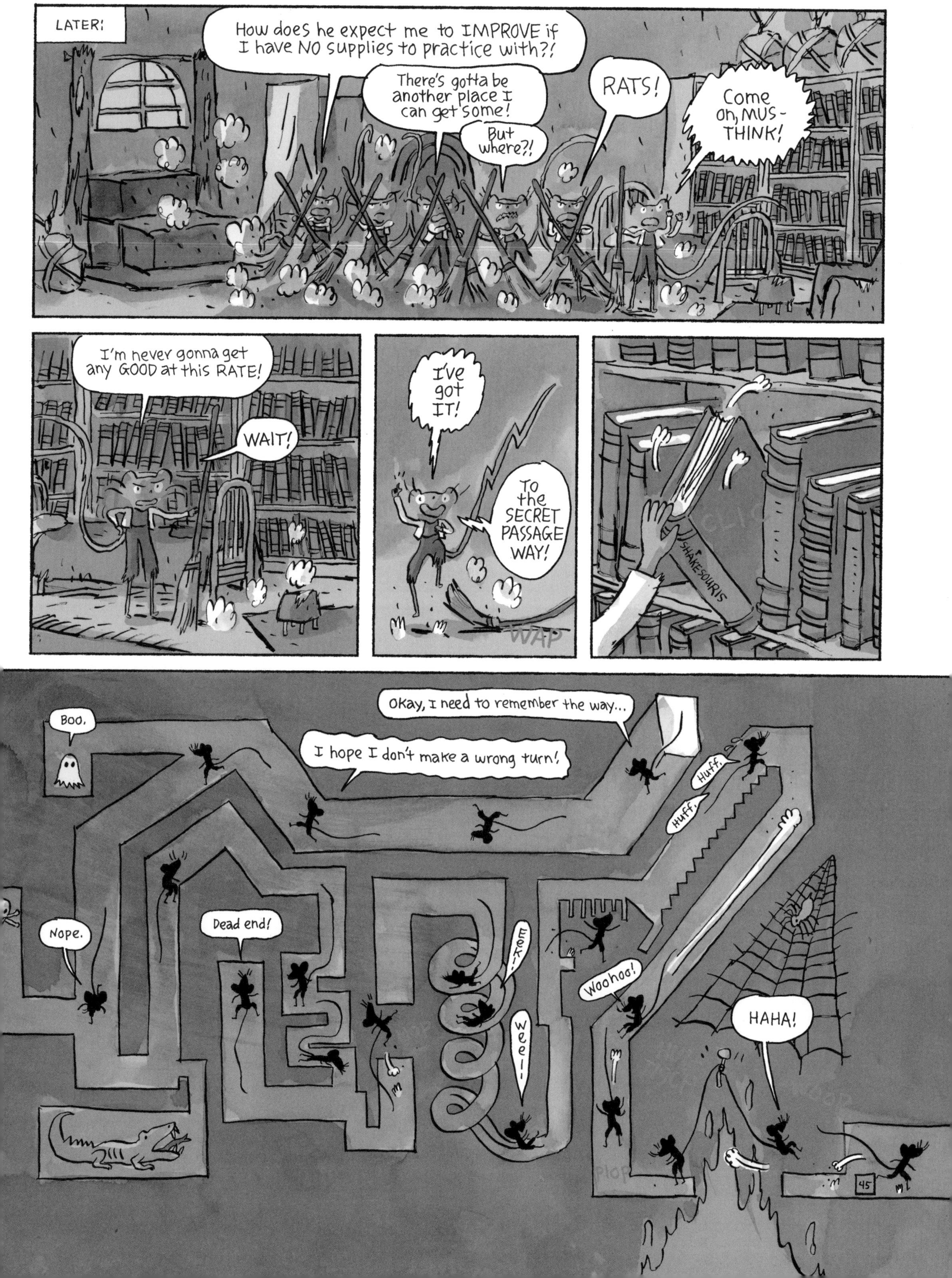
LATER:
How does he expect me to IMPROVE if I have NO supplies to practice with?!
There's gotta be another place I can get some!
But where?!
RATS!
Come on, MUS- THINK!
I'm never gonna get any GOOD at this RATE!
WAIT!
I've got IT!
To the SECRET PASSAGE WAY!
WAP
SHAKESOURIS
Okay, I need to remember the way...
I hope I don't make a wrong turn!
Boo.
Huff.
Huff.
Nope.
Dead end!
Eek!
Wee!
Woohoo!
HAHA!
Plop
45

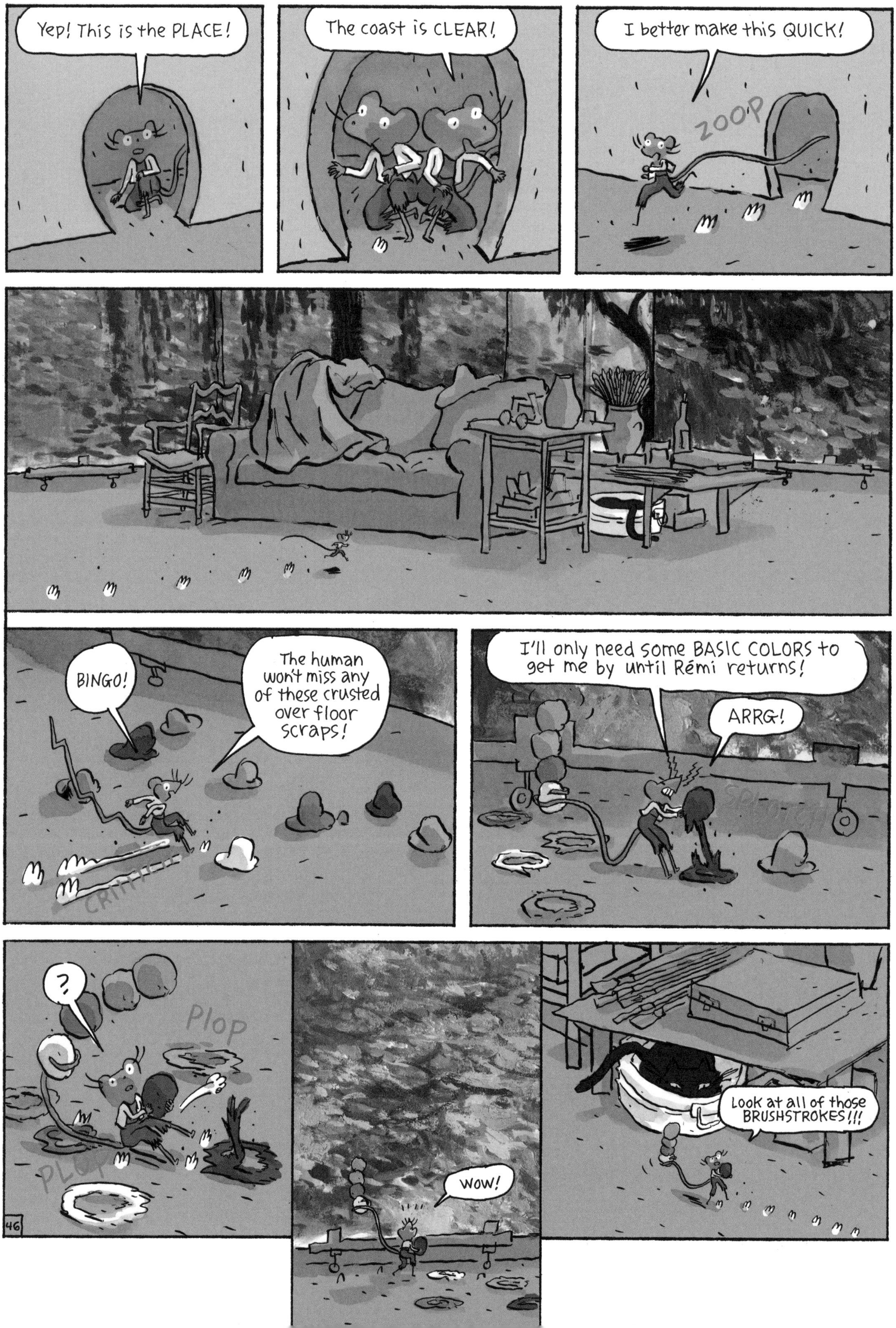
Yep! This is the PLACE!
The coast is CLEAR!
I better make this QUICK!
ZOOP
BINGO!
The human won't miss any of these crusted over floor scraps!
I'll only need some BASIC COLORS to get me by until Rémi returns!
ARRG!
?
PLOP
WOW!
Look at all of those BRUSHSTROKES!!!

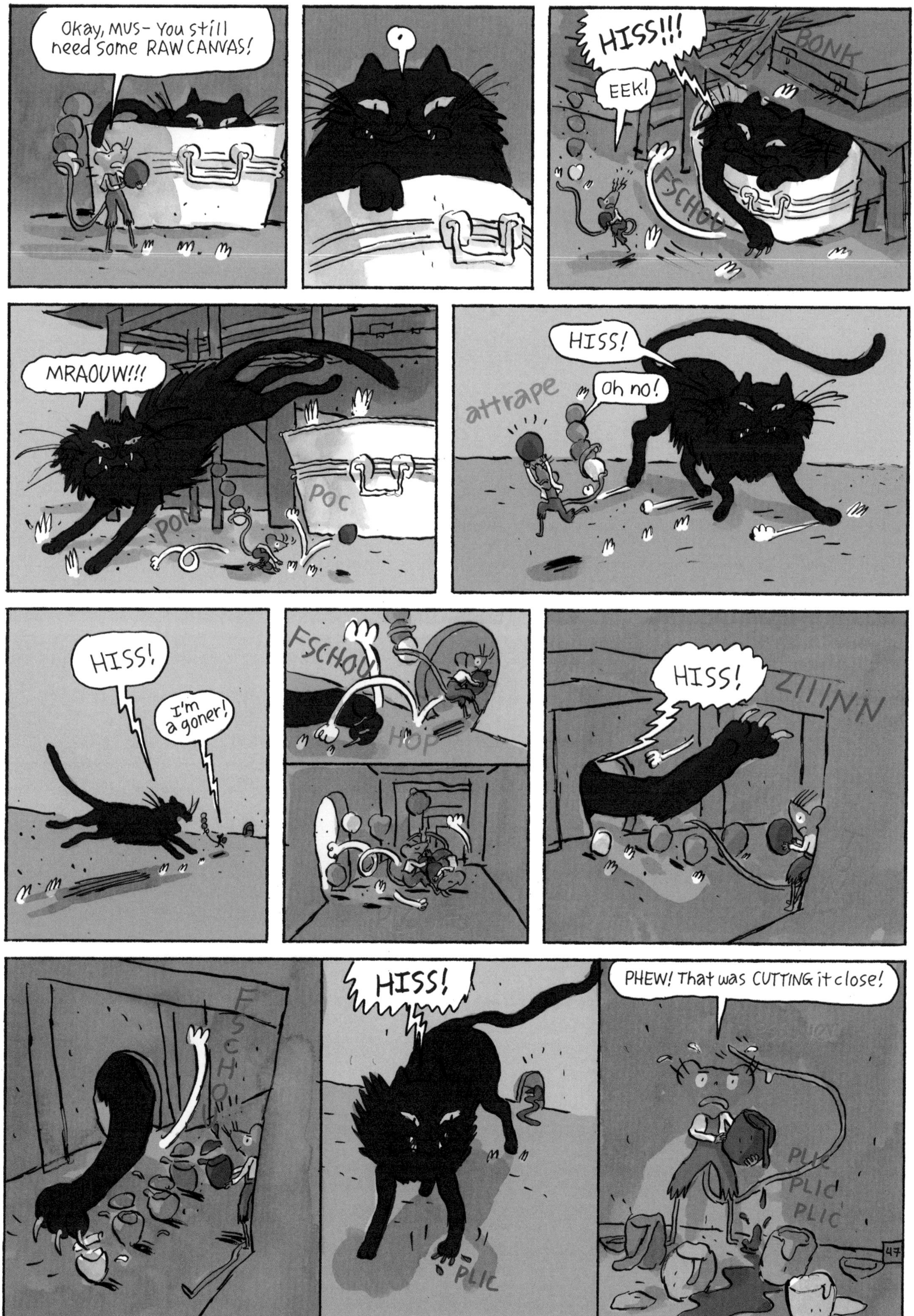
Okay, MUS- You still need some RAW CANVAS!
!
HISS!!!
BONK
EEK!
FSCHOU
MRAOUW!!!
POC
HISS!
Oh no!
attrape
HISS!
I'm a goner!
FSCHOU
HOP
HISS!
ZIIINN
FSCHO
HISS!
PLIC
PHEW! That was CUTTING it close!
PLIC
PLIC
PLIC

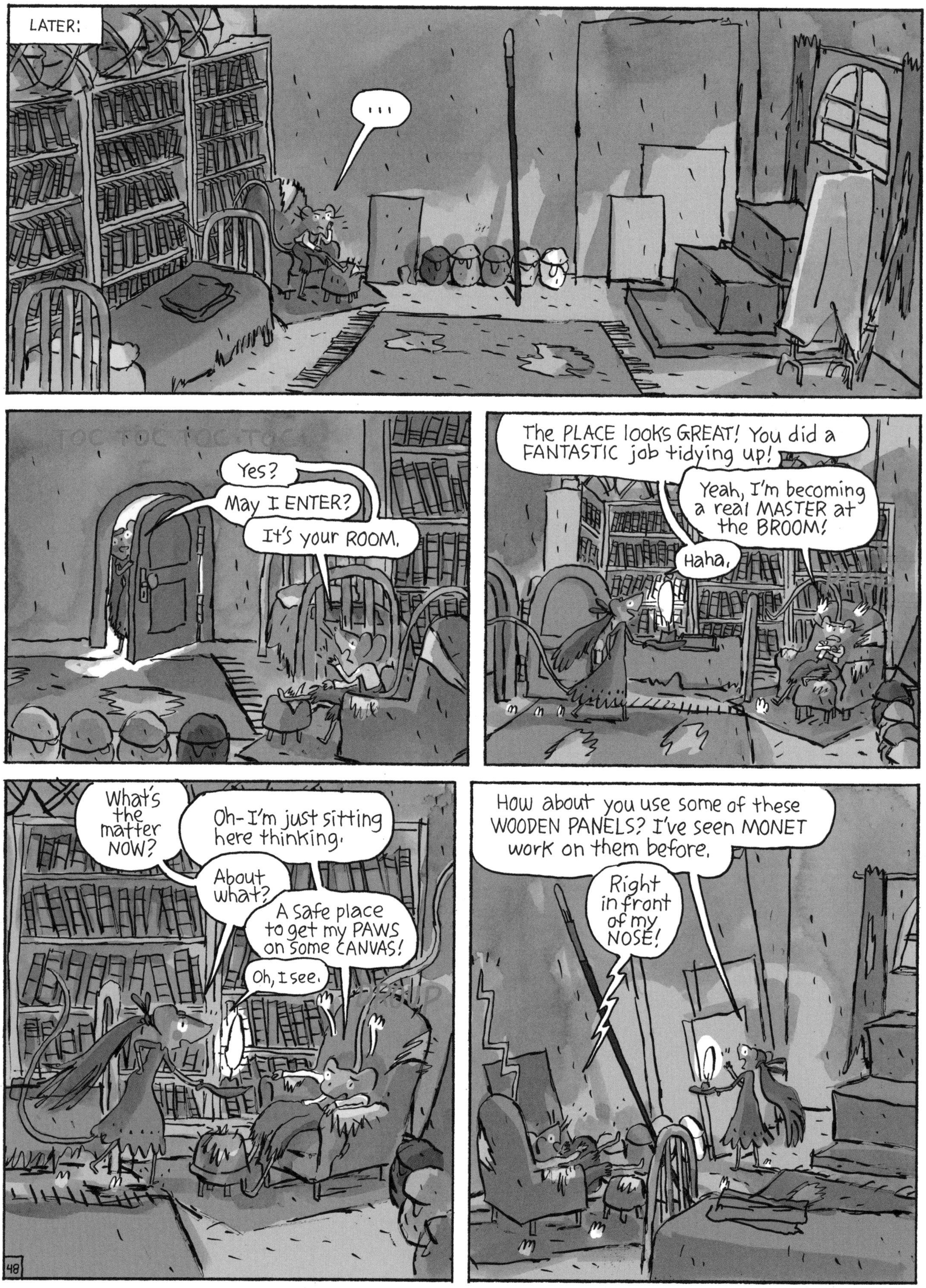
LATER:
...
TOC TOC TOC TOC
Yes?
May I ENTER?
It's your ROOM.
The PLACE looks GREAT! You did a FANTASTIC job tidying up!
Yeah, I'm becoming a real MASTER at the BROOM!
Haha.
What's the matter NOW?
Oh- I'm just sitting here thinking.
About what?
A safe place to get my PAWS on some CANVAS!
Oh, I see.
48
How about you use some of these WOODEN PANELS? I've seen MONET work on them before.
Right in front of my NOSE!

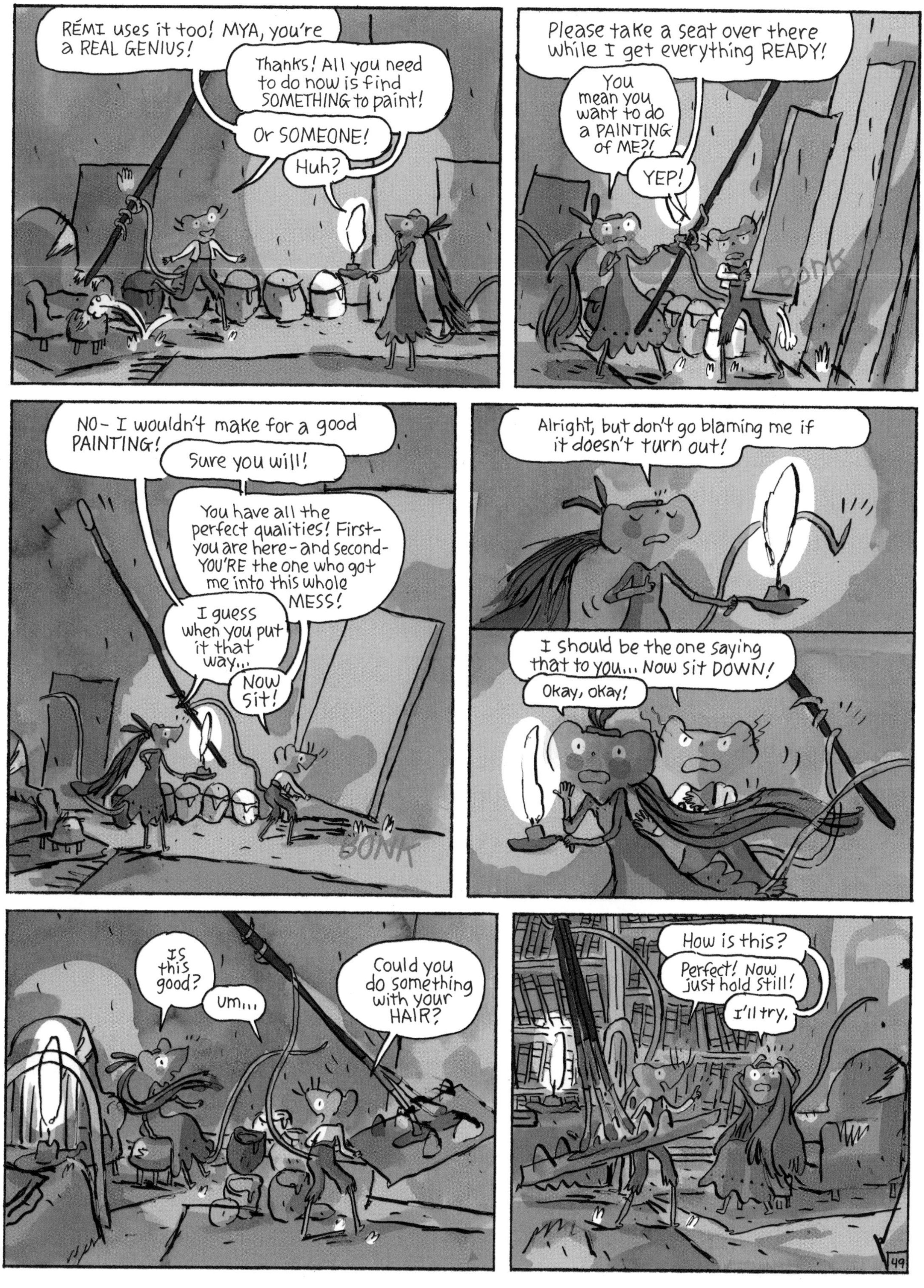

RÉMI uses it too! MYA, you're a REAL GENIUS!
Thanks! All you need to do now is find SOMETHING to paint!
Or SOMEONE!
Huh?
Please take a seat over there while I get everything READY!
You mean you want to do a PAINTING of ME?!
YEP!
BONK
NO- I wouldn't make for a good PAINTING!
Sure you will!
You have all the perfect qualities! First- you are here- and second- YOU'RE the one who got me into this whole MESS!
I guess when you put it that way...
Now sit!
BONK
Alright, but don't go blaming me if it doesn't turn out!
I should be the one saying that to you... Now sit DOWN!
Okay, okay!
Is this good?
Um...
Could you do something with your HAIR?
How is this?
Perfect! Now just hold still!
I'll try.
49

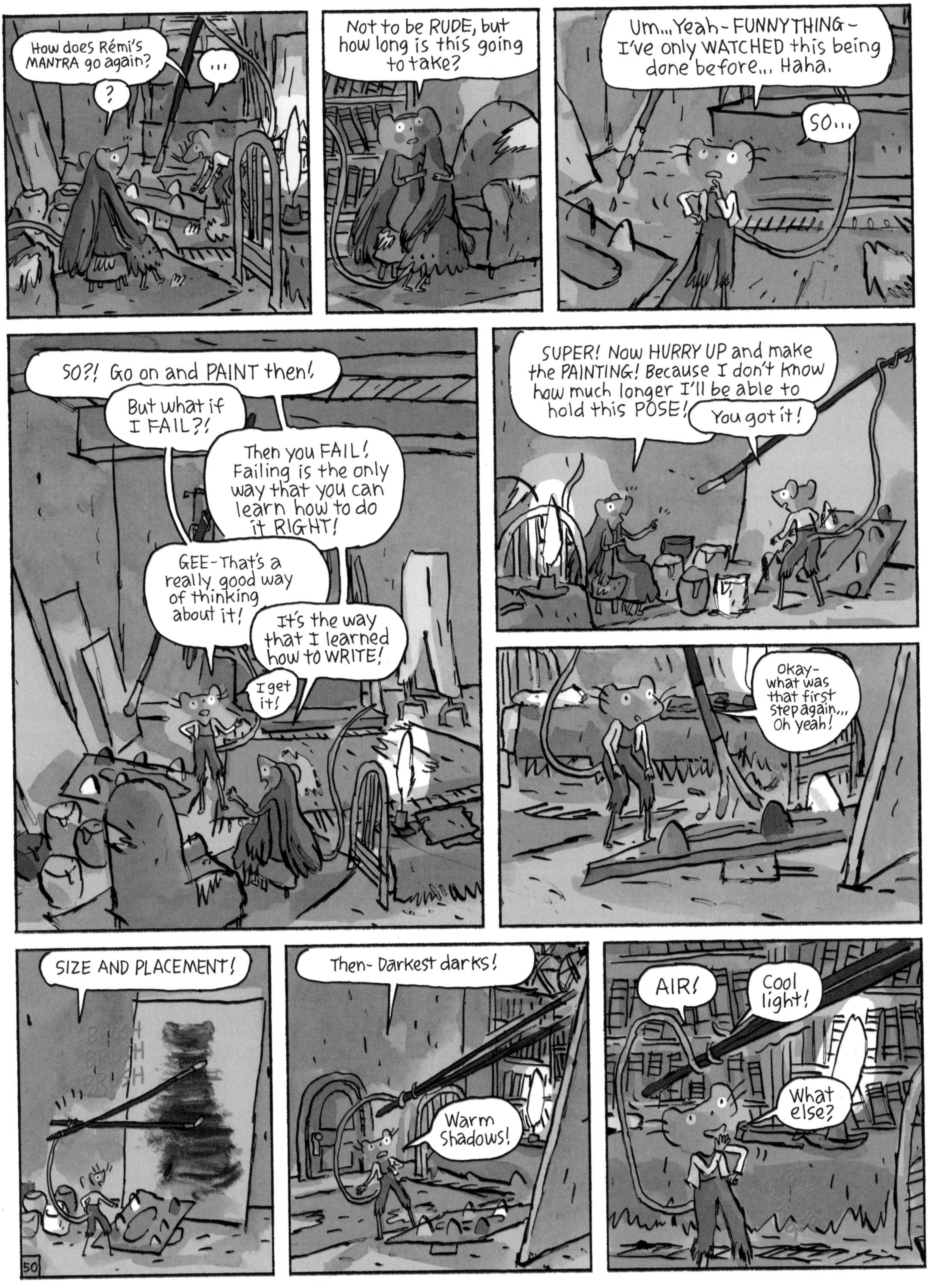
How does Rémi's MANTRA go again?
?
...
Not to be RUDE, but how long is this going to take?
Um... Yeah - FUNNYTHING - I've only WATCHED this being done before... Haha.
SO...
SO?! Go on and PAINT then!
But what if I FAIL?!
Then you FAIL! Failing is the only way that you can learn how to do it RIGHT!
GEE-That's a really good way of thinking about it!
It's the way that I learned how to WRITE!
I get it!
SUPER! Now HURRY UP and make the PAINTING! Because I don't know how much longer I'll be able to hold this POSE!
You got it!
Okay- what was that first step again... Oh yeah!
SIZE AND PLACEMENT!
BRUSH
BRUSH
BRUSH
50
Then- Darkest darks!
Warm Shadows!
AIR!
Cool light!
What else?

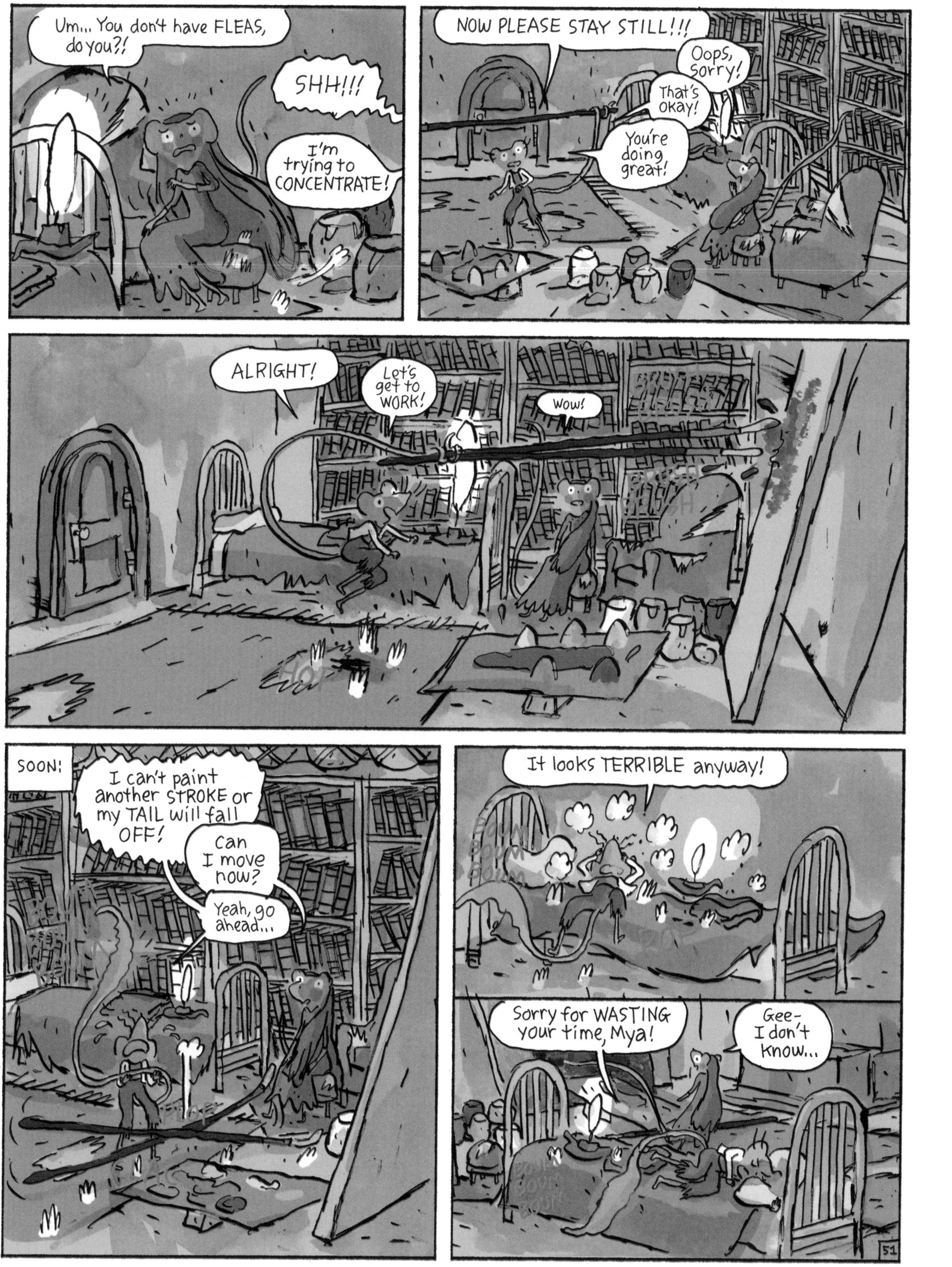

Um... You don't have FLEAS, do you?!
SHH!!!
I'm trying to CONCENTRATE!
NOW PLEASE STAY STILL!!!
Oops, sorry!
That's okay!
You're doing great!
ALRIGHT!
Let's get to WORK!
Wow!
SOON:
I can't paint another STROKE or my TAIL will fall OFF!
Can I move now?
Yeah, go ahead...
It looks TERRIBLE anyway!
Sorry for WASTING your time, Mya!
Gee- I don't know...
51

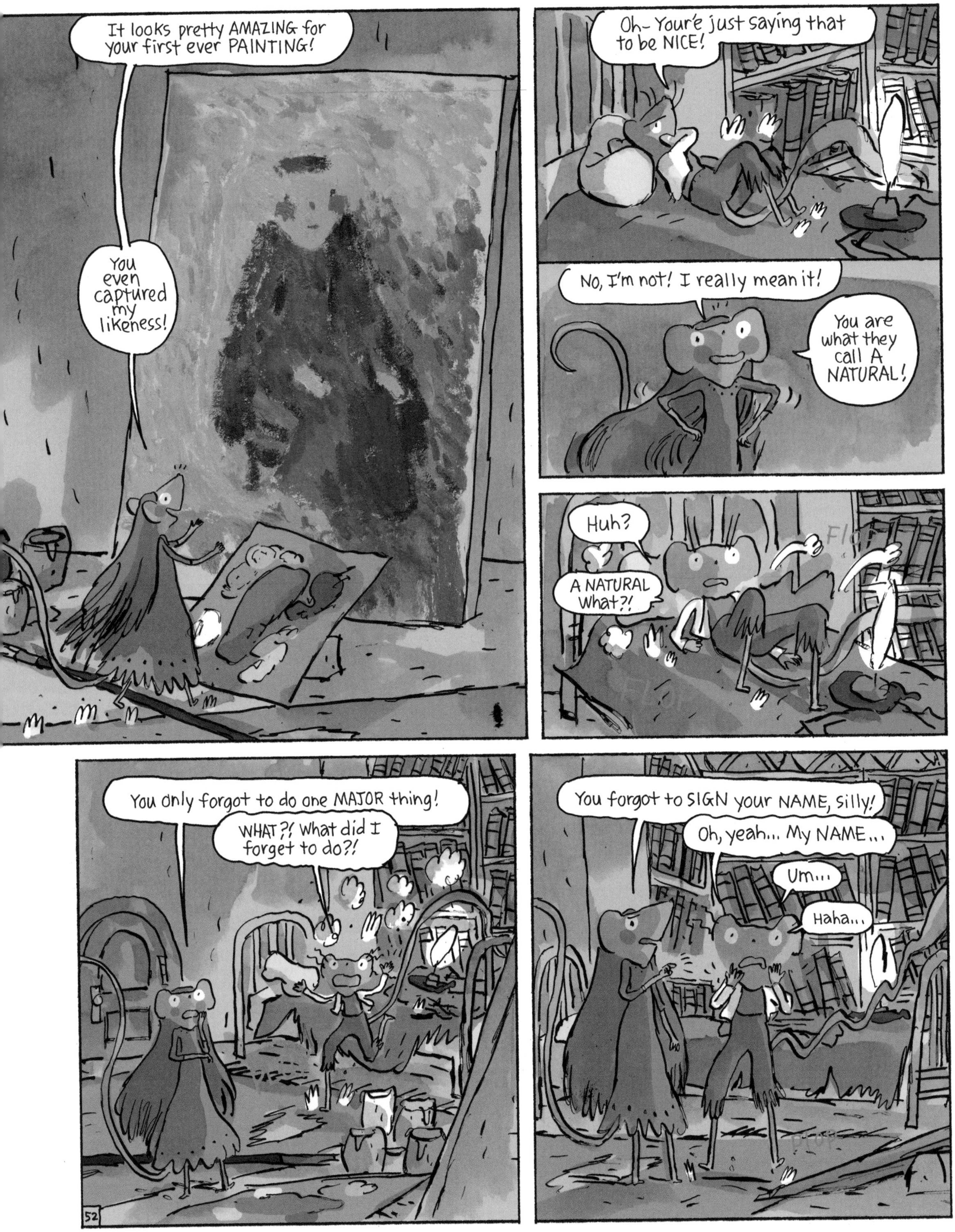
It looks pretty AMAZING for your first ever PAINTING!
You even captured my likeness!
Oh- Your'e just saying that to be NICE!
No, I'm not! I really mean it!
You are what they call A NATURAL!
Huh?
A NATURAL What?!
You only forgot to do one MAJOR thing!
WHAT?! What did I forget to do?!
You forgot to SIGN your NAME, silly!
Oh, yeah... My NAME...
Um...
Haha...
52

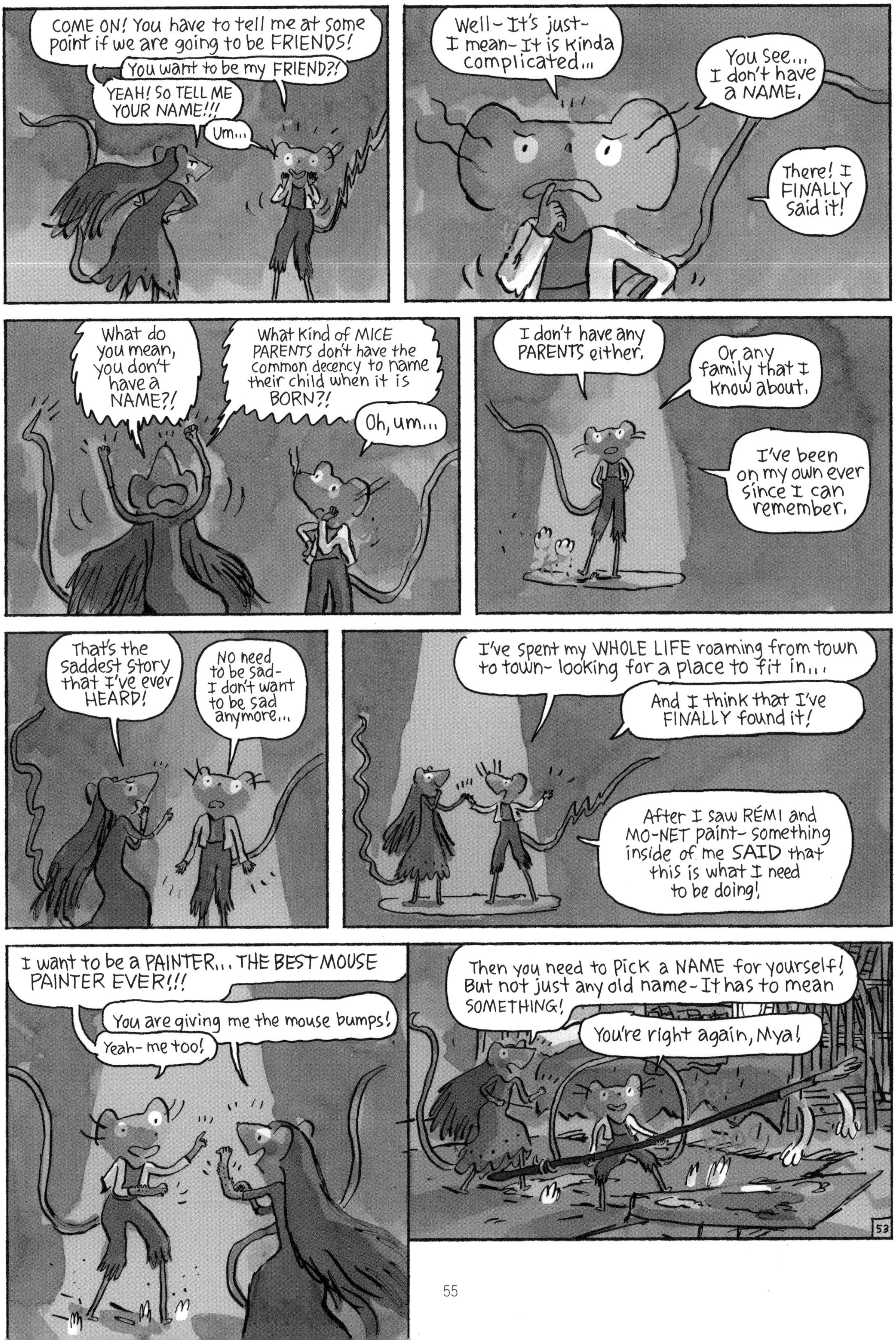
COME ON! You have to tell me at some point if we are going to be FRIENDS!
You want to be my FRIEND?!
YEAH! SO TELL ME YOUR NAME!!!
Um...
Well- It's just- I mean- It is kinda complicated...
You see... I don't have a NAME.
There! I FINALLY said it!
What do you mean, you don't have a NAME?!
What kind of MICE PARENTS don't have the common decency to name their child when it is BORN?!
Oh, um...
I don't have any PARENTS either.
Or any family that I know about.
I've been on my own ever since I can remember.
That's the saddest story that I've ever HEARD!
No need to be sad- I don't want to be sad anymore...
I've spent my WHOLE LIFE roaming from town to town- looking for a place to fit in...
And I think that I've FINALLY found it!
After I saw RÉMI and MO-NET paint- something inside of me SAID that this is what I need to be doing!
I want to be a PAINTER... THE BEST MOUSE PAINTER EVER!!!
You are giving me the mouse bumps!
Yeah- me too!
Then you need to pick a NAME for yourself! But not just any old name- It has to mean SOMETHING!
You're right again, Mya!
53

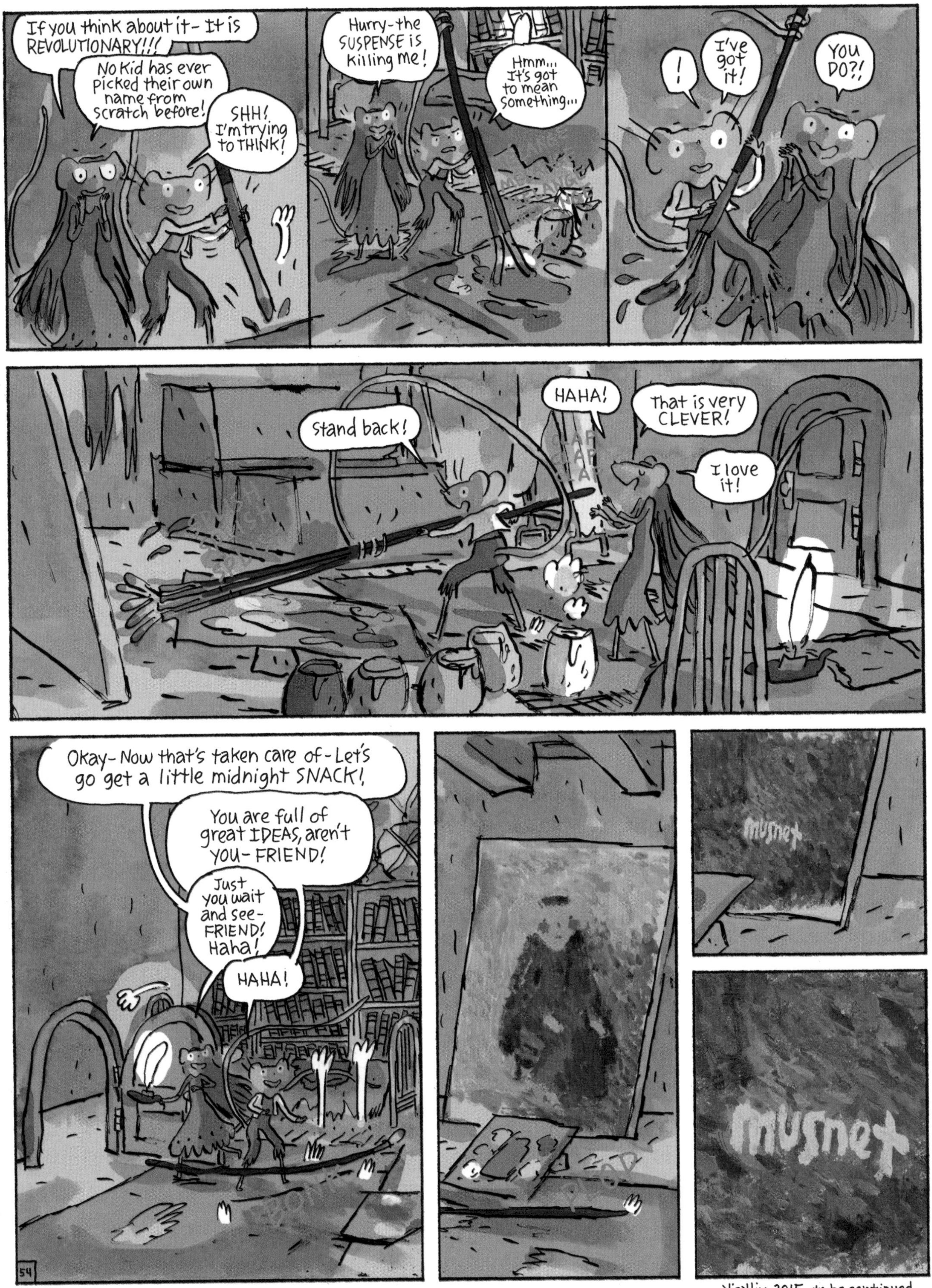
If you think about it- It is REVOLUTIONARY!!!
No Kid has ever picked their own name from scratch before!
SHH! I'm trying to THINK!
Hurry-the SUSPENSE is Killing me!
Hmm... It's got to mean something...
!
I've got it!
YOU DO?!
Stand back!
HAHA!
That is very CLEVER!
I love it!
Okay- Now that's taken care of- Let's go get a little midnight SNACK!
You are full of great IDEAS, aren't YOU- FRIEND!
Just you wait and see- FRIEND! Haha!
HAHA!
54
musnet
musnet

kicklik 2015 to be continued...